"I shall escort you everywhere you ought to be seen."

Ravenham spoke equably as he expertly handled the ribbons of the high-perch phaeton.

"By the end of May, we can consider this matter at an end. You should be quite firmly established by then, I imagine, and should do very well for yourself." His tone was cynical and Gabriella coloured uncomfortably.

"I wish you to know that I had no part in this whatsoever, Your Grace! My opinion was not sought before this—agreement—was entered upon. If it had been, I would have refused, I assure you!"

"But you do not draw back now, I notice," he drawled.

"Your Grace, you may consider yourself released from any obligation to me or my family as of this moment!" she exclaimed hotly. "Pray return me to my sister's house at once!"

"If that is your wish," Ravenham replied, turning the horses. "We cannot, however, end this agreement yet. I have never been a man to go back on his word, and do not intend to change now. I have not yet paid my losses."

GABRIELLA
BRENDA HIATT

Harlequin Books

TORONTO • NEW YORK • LONDON
AMSTERDAM • PARIS • SYDNEY • HAMBURG
STOCKHOLM • ATHENS • TOKYO • MILAN
MADRID • WARSAW • BUDAPEST • AUCKLAND

For my husband, Keith,
who believed in me when I didn't

Published March 1992

ISBN 0-373-31170-2

GABRIELLA

CHAPTER ONE

"GABRIELLA, I INSIST," said Mrs. Gordon firmly, smoothing out the letter which lay before her on the breakfast table and flicking an imaginary crumb off its well-perused surface. "It is extremely kind in your sister to make the offer at all, with you already past the usual age for a girl making her come-out in Society."

"An offer she has been most persistent in making these three years past," replied the girl across from her, impatiently winding a strand of her long, golden brown hair about one slim wrist. "You know very well that it was never my wish, nor Papa's, that I accept one of Angela's invitations."

"It is my wish, however," snapped her mother, "and your papa, being dead, God rest his soul, no longer has any say in the matter."

"And that's another thing, Mama," continued Gabriella in a carefully reasonable tone. "I will not yet be out of mourning when the Season starts in May, and so would be unable to attend any of those glittering social functions which Angela describes at such length, even if I were to go." She tried not to sound smug as she delivered what was surely an unanswerable argument.

"Nonsense!" Her mother dismissed such reasoning with a flick of her fingers. "You know as well as I that your papa would never have wanted you to deny yourself pleasure as a way of remembering him. Who in London is to know that he died in July rather than April, unless you see fit to bruit it about? I doubt that Angela will wear mourning through the Season.''

"I rather doubt it, too," responded Gabriella with a touch of sourness that her mother, thankfully, did not notice. She had not seen her sister in nearly five years, even their father's funeral having been unable to drag her from her busy social schedule, and could not remember that young lady ever bowing to any consideration which might interfere with her own pleasure. She could not understand why Angela was so determined in her efforts to present her to the London ton but somehow suspected, from what she knew of her sister, that Angela would find more amusement in the endeavour than she would.

There was no point in telling her mother this, however. Angela had always been the apple of their mother's eye, with her fairylike blonde beauty and cultured airs. Mrs. Gordon had predicted, almost from her birth, that her eldest daughter would go far in the world; nor had she been mistaken. At nineteen, Angela had managed to catch the eye of Sir Seymour Platt, a young and tolerably wealthy baronet, who had married her and whisked her off to London to be (if her letters were to be believed) the reigning toast of the Town, and one of its leading hostesses. Mrs. Gordon was completely unable to fathom how her younger daughter could fail to dream of a similar conquest.

"But what about the practice?" Fifteen-year-old Gabe, whose presence both ladies had hitherto been inadvertently ignoring, broke into the lengthening silence. "We'll never be able to hold on to it if Brie leaves. Why, already more than half of the farmers are sending to Mr. Bennet over in White Rock instead of to us. What about that, Ma?''

Gabriella winced. While grateful for her brother's support, she was well aware that this was hardly the argument which would be likely to sway their mother. Mrs. Gordon had objected, even while her husband was alive, to her daughter's interest and involvement in his veterinary practice, and Brie considered herself lucky that her mother had not gone so far as to forbid her continued involvement in it since his death. What she didn't need right now was Gabe's reminding their mother of her unfeminine interests; if anything, it was likely to strengthen her determination to bundle Gabriella off to London!

"I spoke to Mr. Bennet yesterday," stated Mrs. Gordon calmly, causing both her children to gape at her in astonishment. She had never involved herself in the practice any more than was absolutely necessary, and not at all since their father died. "He has agreed to purchase the practice from us, along with all of your father's medicines and equipment, for a very useful sum. That seemed the wisest course since, if we wait, he will no doubt acquire most of it, anyway, with no compensation to us for poor Gabriel's years of work at building it up."

Gabe and Brie stared at their mother in stricken silence. Brie managed to find her voice first.

"Mother, how could you?" she asked in a horrified whisper. "The practice was to have been Gabe's! You know that was always Papa's intention."

"Your papa, God rest him, expected to carry on the practice himself until Gabe was of an age to become his partner. None of us could have foreseen the accident which took him last year. Why he couldn't have left the dratted lamb on that ledge... But that is over and done. What matters is how we are to live now." Two sets of eyes continued to accuse her, and she straightened her shoulders defensively.

"You said yourself that many of the farmers are already taking their business to White Rock. I fail to see how you thought we could possibly hold the practice together for several more years. Why, Gabe has not even finished his apprenticeship! Which reminds me—Mr. Bennet said if Gabe were to go to school for a year or two, get some formal education, that *he* would be willing to take him on as an assistant afterwards. So it's not as though I had forgotten you." This last was delivered almost pleadingly to her son.

"Perhaps you are right, Mama," said Brie. She was beginning to recover from her shock, though Gabe was still looking rebellious. "I suppose we were deceiving ourselves to think we could go on as before without Papa. The farmers trust me, and Gabe, too, but there is no denying that neither of us is strong enough for the really heavy cases." Her eyes turned to her brother.

"Can you blame them for calling in Bennet for a difficult calving? You know as well as I do that in those cases knowledge is no substitute for plain brute strength." She still felt betrayed by what her mother had done, but had no desire to see a permanent rift in the family because of it. Gabe met her eyes, and some of the tension went out of his face.

"Maybe, so," he said reluctantly. "But I tell you to your head, Ma, that I want no part of being Bennet's assistant. I'll go to school if you want, but I'll apprentice elsewhere. Then maybe I'll come back here and give old Bennet some competition!"

Mrs. Gordon was so relieved to have the dreaded confrontation over that she did not feel disposed to argue with her son. She had been certain that she was doing the right thing, but equally certain that her children would violently disagree with her, and she was quite pleased with herself for successfully diverting the expected storm. It never occurred to her that much of the credit for that was Gabriella's.

"Does Mr. Bennet take over immediately, or are we to have a grace period?" asked Brie, her tone sharp in spite of her efforts at peacemaking.

"We decided on a two-week delay," answered her mother. "That should give *us* time to notify all the farmers of the change and to tie up the loose ends of the business. Now, if you will excuse me, I have correspondence to attend to." She rose swiftly and vacated the room, leaving Brie and Gabe to hash out the details themselves.

"Us!" sputtered Gabe sarcastically. "When has she ever concerned herself with the farmers or any other part of the practice which didn't come right into the house?"

"Now that's not fair," said his sister, though her feelings were much the same. "Don't you remember that pair of kids last spring? Mama went out to the barn to bottle-feed them twice or thrice a day for weeks. I'm not sure she didn't become a bit attached to them."

Gabe snorted. "She only did it because Papa asked her to." He caught his sister's look and relented. "Perhaps she did like the goats a little. But surely you can't think it right that she sold the practice right out from under us without a word!"

"No, I don't think it was right," agreed Brie with a sigh, "but I have to admit I can see why she did it. She knew we would never have agreed to it if she had asked us, though it has been increasingly obvious, even to me, that we really cannot handle it ourselves. Oh! I miss Papa so!" Her large turquoise blue eyes suddenly glistened with unshed tears, as her loss overwhelmed her again, as it did at odd moments.

Now it was Gabe's turn to take charge, showing a maturity beyond his years. "There, there, Brie, I miss him, too," he said, patting her shoulder comfortingly. "What we need to do right now, though, is work out which of us will go to which farms to spread the word. And, who knows? Maybe I'll like going to school! Where do you think I should go?"

These topics successfully diverted his sister from her incipient tears, and they fell to making plans for the day, the week and the year to come. Both carefully avoided the subject of Angela's invitation, although Brie knew her mother had by no means forgotten it and would bring it up again at the first opportunity.

In this she was not mistaken. Two days later, Gabe having left them alone while he went to help at a protracted lambing, Mrs. Gordon cornered her daughter in their small parlour and reintroduced the topic. This time she was well prepared, strategically outlining the advantages which would accrue to the whole family as a result of Gabriella's debut, and systematically overriding every objection brought forward. Brie's final defence was that she felt certain her father would not have approved, but her mother waved that consideration aside again.

"He only refused before because he needed you here in the spring to help with the birthings," she asserted, contrary to what Brie believed to be the truth. "Besides, you must remember his saying that one of these years you should go. This must be the year, before you are old enough to be considered a spinster."

"Surely, twenty is too old already," said Brie, but without much spirit. She knew her mother had won. Her mother knew it, too, and fell happily to discussing the particulars of Gabriella's debut. Her daughter contributed little to the conversation, nodding or murmuring when some response on her part seemed called for, but Mrs. Gordon apparently had no fault to find with her subdued manner and continued to plan aloud.

"Angela will no doubt take you shopping at once, and you may trust to her excellent taste to outfit you in style. To fill the gap, we can have one or two of my old things altered to fit you, I suppose."

As soon as she could break away, Brie threw on a shawl and climbed to her favourite "thinking spot," a low hill crowned by a flat stone outcropping within sight of the house. Watching her progress from a window, her mother marvelled again at the difference between her two daughters.

Angela had never been difficult to understand. Her dreams had been those of any normal young lady: a good match and a life of leisure. Those had been Mrs. Gordon's dreams also, when she had married Gabriel Gordon, second son of Viscount Chapin. While she had never admitted it to herself, and certainly would never have wished for her brother-in-law's death, it had nonetheless been in the back of her mind that he might conceivably die without heir, leaving the title and the comfortable estate that went with it to her husband.

That, of course, had never come to pass. Instead, it was Gabriel who had died, while his brother had two healthy sons. The families had not been close, though once or twice, when the children were much younger, they had been invited to visit Lord Chapin and his wife. The journey had been tedious, as the estate was located near the Scottish border, and Lady Chapin had treated Mrs. Gordon, who was herself granddaughter to an earl, with such condescension that the connection had been all but dropped.

Mrs. Gordon had truly loved her husband, however, and, once resigned that she would never be a viscountess, had drawn what contentment she could from her lot in life, especially when the opportunity to live out her girlish dreams through Angela presented itself. Her eldest daughter's letters, although more infrequent than she could wish, were ever a source of delight to her and proudly circulated among her few friends in the district. It rankled somewhat that an invitation to herself was never included, but with both girls in London, she hoped that oversight might soon be remedied.

Gabriella, though, had always been a puzzle to her mother. She seemed to want no more out of life than to spend her days tramping round the nearby farms and few estates tending to sick animals—hardly a fit occupation for a lady! And a lady she was—Mrs. Gordon had seen to that. Brie could stitch, draw, play the pianoforte and speak French with the best of them, though one would never guess it to look at her. A Season in London would be the very thing for her. It would take her mind off of her un-ladylike pursuits and turn them into proper channels. She felt she could trust Angela to see to that.

Seated atop the knoll, Brie was also considering her coming Season in London, though with considerably less complacency. These rolling Cotswold Hills in northern Gloucestershire had held a firm grip on her heart for as long as she could remember, as had the animals she had grown to know and love during her years of immersion in her father's veterinary practice. Of course, there would be plenty of horses in London, and perhaps a few dogs, but she would hardly be allowed to concern herself with them. And what of the sheep and cows which dotted the beautiful landscape here?

It would only be for two months, she reminded herself. Then, no matter what arguments Mama and Angela put forth, she would return to this, her true home. She drew her knees up to her chin and gazed lovingly at the small manor house and its attendant outbuildings; more than a farm, but not quite an estate, it had always been the centre of her world. They received rent from some half dozen farmers, but their real income had come from her father's practice. Where was it to come from now? Her mother had not named a sum, but Brie doubted that what Mr. Bennet might be willing to pay would support them indefinitely.

The sun had set, flinging its last bright rays across the evening sky in a beautiful panorama which Brie never tired of watching. As the air grew cooler, she drew her thick hair, which grew past her waist, about her shoulders as a second shawl. Papa had always loved her hair, she recalled fondly, and had always overruled Mama when she insisted that it was high time it was cut. Her glory, he had called it. Brie herself had always considered it her one and only claim to beauty.

Flinging the golden brown mass behind her, she stood up, recognising Gabe's tuneless whistle as he returned from Mr. Donelly's farm. She ran lightly down the hill to question him about the lambing, her glory streaming out behind her.

"How did you fare?" she asked as she reached the bottom, though she knew that if any lambs had died her brother would not be whistling.

"Well enough, but some work to it," replied Gabe with a smile. "Old Donelly had been trying and trying to get that lamb to come. Turned out that lamb was twins, and he had the nose of one lying on the hind feet of the other. Of course they wouldn't budge!"

Brie chuckled along with him. "I wish I'd been there instead of here," she said wistfully.

"Ma still on at you?" asked Gabe in quick concern. It wasn't like Brie to sound so despondent.

"I'm afraid so. Worse, I've finally given in. Without the practice to keep up, I don't have much reason to hold out anymore."

"Oh, Brie!" Gabe gave her a startled glance. "But London—you know what Papa always used to say: that all the wickedest people in England are gathered there."

"But he let Angela go," replied Brie defensively, although Gabe was only echoing her own thoughts.

"Only after she and Mother plagued him to death about it. He always did give in to Mother about Angela, you know. But it was different with you."

That was true. There had always been a special closeness between Brie and her father, and she had drawn her view of the world, and life, from him rather than from her mother.

"Besides," said Gabe, as if his words were decisive, "Papa always said that we could never be as truly happy in London as we are here." He had disagreed with his father on that point, but it was a convenient one to bring up now.

"Yes, but he also said it was up to us to make our own happiness in this world. If I stand by everything he taught us, I suppose I can work at that in London as well as here," she said with a sigh. "Besides, it's only for two months." That thought was rapidly becoming a talisman against her dread of the great city.

"You know, I'll wager London ain't half so bad as Papa always painted it," said Gabe, changing his position suddenly after a moment's thought. "Do you suppose Angela would let me come, too?"

"I wouldn't think so, Gabe. She has never mentioned it, at any rate. Besides," she said more forcefully as a sudden thought struck her, "if you came, Mama would certainly come, as well, and then she and Angela would conspire against our ever returning to the country. You know Mama always said she preferred Town life and only agreed to live here for Papa's sake."

"She wouldn't sell the manor and all without telling us, would she?" asked Gabe in sudden alarm.

"She can't," replied Brie simply. "It is entailed, which means it is yours by right—and you can't sell it, either," she concluded with some satisfaction.

"As if I would!" exclaimed her brother, obviously hurt that she could think him capable of such villainy.

"Come on," said Brie, taking his arm and steering him towards the house. "You must be famished. Tell me all about the lambing."

Chatting comfortably about the subject dearest to both of their hearts, the two young Gordons turned the corner of the house to enter the well-lighted kitchen at the rear.

CHAPTER TWO

LADY PLATT PUT ASIDE the letter from her mother with mixed feelings. She supposed she should be glad that little Gabriella was finally going to accept her kind offer to bring her out, but after three years of asking and being refused she had become complacent about doing the proper thing—offering—without having to go to the trouble of following through.

Basically a selfish person, Angela had only offered in the first place because it had come to her well-shaped ears that she was acquiring a reputation for hardheartedness. And all undoubtedly because of her public set-down to that callow Mr. Jenkins, who had been driving her to distraction with his declarations of undying love! Well, he had certainly deserved it; he had begun to take up time she would much rather have spent with more agreeable admirers.

It occurred to her if the world could see how generous and kind she was to sponsor her poor, homely little sister into Society that such unjust rumours would be overset. And who could tell? It was even conceivable (albeit barely) that Gabriella might make a creditable match and draw off their mother's increasingly broad hints about money troubles.

Angela told herself that these reasonings held as good now as they had three Seasons ago. She hated to admit it, but her position in Society had slipped a bit lately and

could use just this sort of boost. Perhaps Lady Jersey
would even take one of her eccentric likings to Gabriella
and forgive Angela the criticism she had made (with the
kindest intentions, of course!) about that lady's dreadful
purple turban the spring before last. The Platts' vouchers
to Almack's had somehow failed to be renewed after that
little incident, a situation Angela would give much to
remedy. Rising gracefully, she rang for the housekeeper.

"Mrs. Madsen," she said decisively when that worthy
arrived, "my sister Gabriella will be joining us in a week's
time to make her bows to Society. Pray have the maids
prepare the Blue Room for her stay." There! she said to
herself, as the housekeeper left to carry out her orders. No
one was going to accuse Lady Angela Platt of hardheartedness *this* Season!

THE MONTH OF APRIL had fairly flown by, it seemed to
Brie, as she bounced along with the other passengers on
the London-bound stage. There had been so much to do
over the past weeks, what with turning over their records
to Mr. Bennet and reassuring each individual farmer that
his stock would still receive the best of care (which she devoutly hoped would be true), that there had really been no
time for the nervousness she had expected as the date of
her debut drew near.

Perhaps it was just as well that she was already on her
way, she mused. After all, the more quickly she got this
wretched Season out of the way, the more quickly she
could return home. She resolutely refused to consider what
she would do at home now, with the practice out of their
hands.

Looking ahead to the Season in London, Brie bent her
thoughts to how she could most profitably use her time
there. She had already promised Gabe that she would put

in a good word for him with anyone she met that might conceivably have influence at one of the schools. That must be her first concern, obviously. She foresaw no difficulty there; after all, how much time could parties, balls and the theatre possibly consume? No doubt she would have ample time left over to devote to the arrangements of Gabe's schooling.

Brie looked out of the coach window at the passing scenery; they had now passed beyond the environs known to her, and the countryside was subtly changing. In spite of herself, she felt an unexpected surge of excitement at the thought of experiencing the new and unknown.

She glanced over at Molly, her mother's maid, who had come along for propriety's sake and was to return to Gloucestershire once her mistress's daughter was settled in at Lady Platt's. Brie could only be glad that the maid had finally fallen asleep, as her incessant chatter had prevented any thought on her own part and revealed a lack of any such ability on Molly's part.

"Are we 'most there yet, Miss Brie?" she had asked less than half an hour ago.

"No, of course not, Molly," Brie had replied with a laugh. "We've only been on the road a few hours and it is at least a two-day journey to London. We shall be spending the night at some inn or other and shall continue on in the morning. If the distance were so short, I daresay Mama would have consented to let me come alone."

Molly had merely nodded, unembarrassed, and continued to describe every object they passed as though the other occupants of the coach were blind. "There's less trees now than there was," she announced, "and the land is flatter. The roof on that there stone barn is rotted out. Someone ought to see to fixing it." On and on she had rattled, but finally, mercifully, her voice had dropped to a murmur and then to silence as the swaying of the coach rocked her to sleep.

The sun was setting when the stage stopped for the night at a large posting house and inn proclaimed to be the Ruby Crown by a gaudily painted sign hanging above the front entrance. Brie wakened Molly, who had continued to doze fitfully, before stepping from the coach to stretch her cramped limbs. After speaking with the coachman to ascertain the time that their journey would continue in the morning, she took the groggy maid by the arm and proceeded into the inn in search of sustenance and a room for the night.

Having bespoken a meal in the common room in an hour's time (the private parlour, the innkeeper had proudly informed her, was already engaged by one of the nobility) and having sent Molly up to the room they were to share, Brie wandered back outside to pass the time until dinner. Irresistibly, she was drawn to the rear of the inn, where the stables were located, along with a small piggery and poultry yard. She watched the antics of a large litter of pigs for several minutes, laughing aloud as they cavorted and tumbled about the sty. No one paid her the least bit of attention; dressed for travelling as she was in her serviceable brown homespun, she might easily have passed for one of the menials employed at the inn.

She was just turning to go back inside, as the dusk was deepening, when she noticed a smartly liveried groom leading a horse in such appalling condition that she instinctively paused for a closer look. The animal had once been a fine bay gelding, its superior breeding still showing in the well-shaped head and legs. Now, however, the poor creature was little more than a walking skeleton, while welts and cuts showed that it had been severely beaten as well as starved. Without stopping to consider the

fact that no one here knew anything of her background
with animals, she rounded angrily on the unsuspecting
groom.

"This kind of abuse is an outrage!" she fairly shouted
in his startled face. "Anyone who would treat a horse like
this has no business owning one!" The groom began to
stammer some response, but Brie would listen to no excuses. "Take me to your master at once and he shall be
told what ought to be done about people who find it
amusing to mistreat the poor creatures that trust to them
for care."

Shrugging helplessly, the groom led her through the inn
to the door of the private parlour, where he tapped diffi-
dently. His Grace might not welcome an interruption, but
he was not about to try again to reason with this fire-
breathing termagant. He would leave that to his master. As
the parlour door opened, the groom cravenly fled to the
kitchens.

"Yes, what is it?" The man who stood before her was
obviously the "one of the nobility" the innkeeper had referred to, so proclaimed by the fashionable and expensive
cut of his midnight blue coat, the fall of his neckcloth and
the studied disorder of his curling brown hair. He was very
tall, very handsome and, apparently, very impatient. The
cause for that impatience lounged seductively on a sofa
behind him: a plump, raven-haired beauty in an outrageously low-cut red satin gown. This deterred Brie not at
all; in fact, in her anger, she scarcely noticed the woman.

"I have been informed that you are the owner of the bay
gelding out back which is at death's door owing to your
abuse, or that of your underlings," she stated without
preamble, her chin held high. "I wish to tell you, as apparently no one yet has, that such treatment of a poor
dumb beast is inexcusable. I would not have thought any-

one with the pretension to consider himself a gentleman
could be capable of such behaviour!''

At another time, this particular gentleman might have
been amused at the situation. Just now, however, he had
been interrupted in the middle of a most promising *tête-à-
tête* with Mademoiselle Monique, whom he had high hopes
of persuading to become his mistress, as her most recent
protector, Lord Gillings, had left the past week for the
Continent. This being the case, he did not feel disposed to
banter words with this obvious nobody at the door. Her
accent was cultured, to be sure, but her manner and attire
appeared to be that of a servant.

"The condition of my horses can hardly be any business of yours, young woman,'' he said in the icy tone
which had frozen more than one presumptuous London
dandy where he stood, and which had never failed to send
its unfortunate target cringing abjectly away. It failed now.

"Preventing cruelty to animals should be everyone's
business!" flared Brie. "You are obviously a man of high
position. Think of the example you are setting, when others see how poorly you treat your beasts. I should think
you would be ashamed! You must have it in your power to
influence a great many people for good or ill, and this is
how you use that power!"

"That will be quite enough!" snapped his lordship,
perilously close to losing his legendary control. His grey
eyes narrowed as he took in the upright little figure before
him. The girl was nothing out of the ordinary, with brown
hair scraped severely back from her freckled brown face—
a common country wench, no doubt! Who did she think
she was to be taking the Duke of Ravenham, undisputed
leader of Society and well known Corinthian, to task for
the treatment of his horses?

"If you feel so strongly about the fate of that gelding, you are free to purchase him. Discuss it with my groom. The price is fifteen pounds six." That, after all, is what he himself had paid for the poor beast not two hours ago to prevent its further abuse by the tinker who had owned it. The girl's expression confirmed his surmise that she was not in possession of such a sum, and he smiled slightly.

"Now I must ask you to take up no more of my time. Good evening." So saying, he shut the door firmly in Brie's affronted face.

She stood irresolute outside the parlour for a few moments, strongly tempted to knock again, but finally deciding against it. She had the disconcerting feeling that she might, just possibly, have been in the wrong but she quickly shrugged it off. The man was simply too arrogant to admit to any fault, she told herself. Suddenly realising the lateness of the hour, Brie went off to the common room for her dinner, still feeling that she should somehow have done more.

The next morning, she awoke well before daylight and her thoughts went immediately to the poor gelding in the stables—and his infuriating master. Moving quietly so as not to wake the sleeping Molly and perhaps provoke a lengthy questioning, she dressed quickly and slipped out of the room.

Brie made her way to the stables without being observed and walked along the length of the low building until she found the stall which housed the maltreated bay. Speaking softly to alert him to her presence without alarming him, she let herself into the box and gently began to examine the horse's wounds. He had obviously been abused over a long period of time, as old, badly healed cuts were visible along with more recent ones. As far as she could tell in the dim light, he had been beaten with whip,

stick and chain! Her temper began to rise again at the
thought of such atrocities, but she quickly forced her mind
back to the task at hand.

Tearing into thin strips the old petticoat she had brought
with her, Brie expertly cleansed the more recent weals and
applied the salve that her father had always used, and
which she was never without. One never knew when one
might come upon an animal (or even a person!) in need of
emergency care, and she had been well trained to be always prepared. She considered stitching one particularly
nasty cut, but regretfully decided it would be too risky
without an assistant to hold the horse's head.

She thought that what little she had been able to do
should at least allow the existing cuts to heal without in-
fection—assuming, of course, that no further abuse occurred! She hoped her little lecture last night might at least
have done that much good. Perhaps the nobleman's lovely
wife, who had overheard the entire exchange, would be
able to influence him to be kinder, although she had not
seemed especially soft-hearted, Brie had to admit. At any
rate, she herself could do no more at present.

She fervently wished she had carried more money with
her on the journey—how she would have loved to throw
fifteen six (preferably all in coins) in that arrogant peer's
face! The memory of his mocking grey eyes had haunted
her dreams, and she hoped that by tending to his poor
horse she would sleep better in future. It would no doubt
be best if she never saw Lord Whatever-His-Name-Was
again.

The inn was astir when Brie returned, and Molly was
frantically looking for her. She quieted the maid's concern with a tale of having stepped out for a breath of air,
then hurriedly broke her fast while Molly ran to fetch her
trunk from upstairs.

"We'd best scurry, miss," she said breathlessly upon reentering the common room. "The trunk is already stowed and the coachman is anxious to start."

"Of course, Molly," replied Brie, drinking the last of her milk. "Did you have a chance to eat?"

"Yes, miss, in the kitchen, while you was out breathin' the air. There's some real handsome servants here, valets and such-like. One in particular, a groom, I think he was—"

"That will be enough." Brie cut her off, knowing that the maid would willingly describe every person she had met in the past four-and-twenty hours if encouraged. "We need to hurry, I believe you said."

THE DUKE OF RAVENHAM was not in happy spirits as he drove back to London some hours later. His negotiations with Mademoiselle Monique had not gone as planned; she was currently experiencing no lack of funds, and obviously wished to wait until she had several offers to choose among. Thus, the closed carriage he had brought in hopes of furthering their acquaintance during the journey back to Town was empty; he held the ribbons himself, as he found it easier to think while his hands were occupied, while his groom was left to lead the poor bay at a walking pace.

Unaccountably, he blamed the interruption by that serving girl, or whatever she was, for his lack of success. She had certainly put him out of humour with her unfounded accusations and her refusal to be put in her place. Small wonder that he could not properly carry on a seduction after such a scene!

Who could she have been, he wondered again. Whatever training she had received had obviously not included a proper respect for her betters; he could still barely believe her effrontery in presuming to lecture him on his care of horseflesh! Perhaps he should have told her the truth at the outset, and so shortened the confrontation, but he had not felt at the time that she deserved that consideration. Now, however, he was feeling the tiniest pang of regret for that omission.

Her dress and appearance had been common, that was true, but she spoke as though she had some degree of intelligence and education. Her spirit and determined love for animals were things he couldn't help but admire, and her eyes, at least, were not quite ordinary. They were well shaped, he recalled, and of a deep turquoise colour which was most unusual.

Perhaps he had been just a bit harsh, the duke decided. If he ever saw the girl again, he would apologise. Though fully aware that such a chance would almost certainly never present itself, he allowed his conscience to be assuaged by this resolution and turned his thoughts back to the more pressing matter of the delectable but undecided Mademoiselle Monique.

CHAPTER THREE

ARRIVING AT THE IMPOSING Platt residence just at tea-time, Brie was shown directly into the front drawing room by Madsen, the Platts' properly portly butler and husband to the worthy housekeeper. She had barely a chance to take in the expensive, if slightly tasteless, clutter of artwork adorning the numerous gilt tables in the large apartment before she was accosted by her sister.

"Dearest, *dearest* Gabriella, here you are at last!" exclaimed Angela in her carefully cultivated, mellow voice. Rising gracefully, she fairly glided across the room to embrace her sister lightly, kissing the air an inch from each cheek, before turning to her companions.

"Ladies, this is my dear sister Gabriella, who is come to stay with me for the Season, as I told you, and who I haven't seen in simply years! Darling, you must make the acquaintance of two of my dearest friends, Lady Mountheath and Mrs. Gresham." Polite murmurs had barely been exchanged before Angela continued. "You must know, when Gabriella and I were children people constantly commented on the likeness between us, and I assure you no two sisters could ever have been closer. Come, darling, and sit here on the sofa with me," she invited, patting the spot as if she were calling a dog.

Brie moved slowly to join her, a bit taken aback at the two bold-faced lies her sister had just told. No one could fail to notice the stark contrast between Angela, with her plump blonde beauty swathed in amethyst silk, and Gabriella's thin, drab brownness, but the two ladies merely smiled politely. Brie suspected that her sister's comment had been uttered for the sole purpose of forcing that comparison.

"Tell me, my dear," said Angela sweetly when Brie was seated, "do you still tramp about the farms among the livestock as you used? You must spend a great deal of time out of doors to have become so brown! How very healthy, to be sure!" The smile she turned on her dear friends clearly communicated that they were not to expect too much from her poor, bucolic sister.

"As a matter of fact, I do," answered Brie, attempting to mimic Angela's tone. "Or, at least I did until a week ago. We've had to sell the practice, I'm afraid, as Gabe and I were unable to keep it up alone. By the way, we missed you at Papa's funeral, my dear, but I understood that you were too busy to attend." Turning to her sister's guests, she began confidentially, "As I'm certain dear Angela has told you, our father was a—"

Angela's face turned a shade pinker, and she hastily stood up. "How thoughtless of me, Gabriella!" she broke in. "You must be quite worn out after your long journey and I have not even allowed you to take off your travelling things, I was so overcome by seeing you again. Madsen!" The hovering butler appeared at the door. "Pray take my poor sister to her room so that she may rest and freshen up a bit. Dinner will be at seven, my dear, as we are going to the theatre tonight. No doubt you will find that quite a treat."

Having been pointedly dismissed, Brie followed Madsen out of the room after politely taking leave of Lady Mountheath and Mrs. Gresham. She was both satisfied and disappointed to find that Angela had not changed in

the least; she had expected that would be the case, and she
now knew the lay of the land, but still, it would have been
nice....

The Blue Room, into which she was presently shown,
was far grander than anything Brie had expected—though
just *what* she had expected she was not certain. The room
was done in every conceivable shade of blue, from the
striped fabric covering the walls to the sky blue counterpane on the large four-poster. The two gilt chairs were up-
holstered in deep royal blue and the carpeting was of a
floral pattern in which turquoise and robin's egg blue pre-
dominated. The total effect was actually rather soothing,
although she knew it would take her some time to become
accustomed to such elegant surroundings.

Crossing to the large window, Brie pulled aside the curtains, which were of the same striped fabric sported by the
walls, and was rewarded by a panoramic view of South
Audley Street. She watched the comings and goings of all
manner of carriages, curricles, phaetons and pedestrians
with interest until a tap on the door pulled her attention
away. Molly entered to hang up Brie's scant wardrobe in
the clothespress and to prattle about everything that she
had seen in Town thus far.

Brie interrupted her before she could describe the various Platt footmen. "Thank you, Molly," she said firmly.
"I believe I will try to rest now. Angela—Lady Platt, that
is—wishes me dressed for dinner and the theatre at seven,
so please return to assist me at six." Brie was just as glad
the maid would be going back to Gloucestershire in a day
or two.

Molly left quickly, and Brie managed to relax somewhat, though not to sleep, and renewed her resolve to give
Angela the benefit of the doubt, in spite of their inauspi-
cious beginning. After all, she *had* given her this lovely

room for the Season, so her intentions, at least, must have
been good, Brie reasoned. She would try to help her sister
to carry them out.

When Molly returned, the two of them surveyed in mutual dismay the six dresses Brie had brought along. None of
them appeared even remotely appropriate for an evening
at the theatre; Brie's wardrobe had always been more
serviceable than fashionable, even by country standards.

"It was Angela's idea that I accompany them tonight,"
said Brie finally, with a slight shrug. "She must have
known I could have nothing suitable as yet, so it is on her
own head if she finds me an embarrassment. I suppose it
will have to be the yellow, Molly. It is the only silk."

She donned the gown with Molly's help, then surveyed
herself critically in the glass. It fit well enough, as it had
been taken in for that purpose before her departure, but
still it was hardly flattering. The dress was an old one—a
very old one—of her mother's and, unfortunately, it
looked it. As if the unfashionable cut of the gown were not
enough, its dull yellow colour made Brie look positively
sallow and seemed to take the sparkle from her eyes.

Turning quickly away from her reflection, she seated
herself at the pretty blue-and-white dressing table and allowed Molly to restore some semblance of order to her
hair—the severe bun again, as Molly was capable of no
other style. Finally, picking up her ivory shawl, which did
not match the gown in the least, and her reticule, which
was too large for fashion, Brie descended to dinner,
pointedly refraining from another look in the mirror.

In the imposing dining room, which was not, Brie
thought, decorated as tastefully as her own chamber, she
was presented to her host, Sir Seymour Platt.

"So this is little Gabriella, all grown up!" he drawled in
the affected nasal whine Brie had done her best to forget.

The overabundance of lace at his throat and wrists, as well
as the rich (and brightly coloured) embroidery of his
waistcoat proclaimed Sir Seymour one of the dandy set.
Raising his quizzing glass to one slightly bleary eye he ex-
amined his sister-in-law curiously.

"No chance to go shopping yet, I take it? You may be
wondering how I could tell," he went on loftily. "Well, I
daresay you could search all of London and not find another chap who knows so much about the current fash-
ions as myself. And that gown, my dear, ain't it! Take the
neckline, for example—"

"Do stop blathering, Seymour," broke in his wife
dampingly. "You must know that I intend to take my sister to the shops before the Season gets under way. Any fool
can see that her gown is atrociously dowdy, but it will do
for the theatre tonight, I daresay, as long as she doesn't
leave the box."

"Of course, dear, er, quite," replied the self-proclaimed
arbiter of fashion, and gave his attention to his soup.

Brie listened with more amusement than embarrassment. It was obvious, if not surprising, that her sister kept
her graceless husband firmly in his place. She wondered
idly how he comported himself when out from under his
wife's watchful eye. Angela's blunt categorisation of her
gown, as accurate as it was tactless, she refused to dwell
on.

Dinner passed slowly, it seemed to Brie, the overly rich
dishes but little lightened by her brother-in-law's aimless
chatter. Finally, as he concluded a maundering tale about
a wager he had won last month, owing entirely to his incredible skill in handling a snuffbox, the ices were cleared
away and the meal was at an end. Leaving Sir Seymour to
his port, she followed her sister out of the room.

"I suppose that *was* the best you could manage for to-night?" enquired Angela in bored tones as they entered the drawing room. Actually, it suited her quite well that Gabriella's first public appearance should be in such a gown. The transformation she intended for her sister would thus be the more obvious, and would prove to all observers that Lady Platt was charity itself. In truth, she rather regretted the money which would have to be spent to make her sister presentable, but if it restored herself to the forefront of Society, no price could be too great.

"It is the only silk I have with me. It was Mama's, as you might possibly remember."

Angela regarded her sister sourly at this reminder of her neglect of the family in recent years.

"Before we go, I thought it best that we have a talk about how you should conduct yourself in Society," she said, changing the subject. "I could not fail to notice you were quite outspoken this afternoon, and I must tell you that such candour is neither necessary nor appreciated among the higher circles, which I had hoped you might aspire to." Her expression indicated that she was now doubtful of such an achievement. "I will undertake to prepare you for the best society, and I tell you to your head that the time and money involved will be no small thing, but your clothes are only a part of the entire effect. It will do your credit no good for it to be generally known that your father was a common farrier. If asked, you may say that he was the second son of Reginald Gordon, Lord Chapin, and leave it at that."

"Papa was not a farrier, and well you know it, Angela," Brie broke in indignantly. "He did very little blacksmith work, and that only as an occasional favour. He was a veterinary surgeon, and proud of his skill, which saved more than one farmer from ruin. I am not at all ashamed of that! Are you?'' She regarded her sister keenly.

''Be that as it may, you may take my word that his profession is not highly regarded among the *haut* ton.'' Angela chose to ignore that last question. ''You will oblige me by not speaking of it again. Nor would it be good form to let on that a full year has not *quite* passed since his death. There are a few high sticklers who might look askance at your participation in the Season before the formal mourning period has passed.''

Brie looked rebellious, and considered commenting on the fact that her father happened also to be Angela's, but decided it would do little good. It was quite true that her sister was going to bear the total expense of her come-out, whatever her motives might be, and equally true that Angela was far wiser in the ways of Society than she was. Though it did some violence to her feelings, she forced herself to be somewhat conciliatory.

''Very well,'' she said finally. ''I will do my best to say nothing which seems likely to embarrass you. Though,'' she continued, with a firm set to her chin, ''if I am asked direct questions I will not undertake to lie.''

Angela supposed she would have to be content with that; she had feared for a moment that Gabriella would refuse outright. Donning her most gracious smile, she said brightly, ''That is settled, then. Let us fetch our wraps, for if we are to catch the first act we must be off directly.''

The theatre was a novel experience for country-bred Brie. Not only had she never seen so many people under one roof before—or, indeed, so many people anywhere—but the variety of dress and manners, from that of the lowliest commoner on the floor to the titled leaders of Society in their boxes, was well worth observing. She almost felt that the play would be superfluous, with such a show already in progress.

Their own box was fairly crowded, as well, rather to Brie's surprise, for she had expected to share it only with the Platts. Mr. and Mrs. Ancroft, a dashing young couple recently married, were introduced to her, and Brie could not help noticing that Mrs. Ancroft, a petite brunette whose face looked suspiciously painted, wore a gown every bit as immodestly cut as Angela's. Also present were three apparently single gentlemen. By far the handsomest of these was Sir Frederick More, a tall, distinguished-looking man with fair hair and a small, clipped mustache. The other two were as dandified and affected as Sir Seymour, and Brie found them more amusing than attractive.

It soon became apparent that the three unattached gentlemen were there for the sole purpose of flirting with the two married ladies, who, as far as Brie could tell, made no effort to discourage their advances. Nor did their husbands seem to take offence at the particular attentions being paid their wives, though Sir Seymour might very well have been too foxed to notice.

Sir Frederick, however, after paying her sister a few outrageous compliments, drifted over to sit next to Brie. "It is lonely, I know, to be so new to Town, Miss Gordon, but I hope you will believe me when I say that a young lady so personable as yourself will have no difficulty making friends quickly."

Brie looked up quickly to encounter Sir Frederick's charming, and surprisingly kind, smile. "Why, thank you, sir," she said in her pleasant, low voice. "You are very perceptive, for I *was* feeling a bit out of things."

"Perfectly understandable," he assured her. "I believe I understood from your sister that you have never been to London before?"

Brie admitted this to be true, and he proceeded to tell her of some of the sights in store for her, as well as to warn her against certain places—and people—that she would be prudent to avoid. As the curtain rose, Sir Frederick lowered his voice but showed no sign of relinquishing his place by her side, which Brie found both flattering and agreeable. There was nothing of the flirtatious in his manner; rather, he seemed genuinely concerned that she should enjoy her stay in Town.

Brie could not know that Sir Frederick was an accomplished judge of women, and had divined immediately which approach would be most likely to win this inexperienced girl's confidence. He had correctly guessed that the suggestive flattery Lady Platt thrived on would only cause her young sister to withdraw into herself like a snail into its shell and conducted himself accordingly.

His solicitude did not escape the notice of the other occupants of the box. While the others were amused at the unusual sight of the notorious Sir Frederick whiling away his time with a rustic schoolroom miss, Lady Platt was less than diverted. For over a year Sir Frederick had been her most devoted admirer, taking her husband's place as escort when Sir Seymour was incapacitated by drink (and taking his place in other ways, some of the more unkind gossips said, though this last was not—as yet—true) and she was ever jealous of any attentions he might bestow on another.

Not that Gabriella could possibly be a serious threat, she thought. Why, just look at her! Not only was her dress atrociously dowdy, but her manner was also completely unsophisticated, and that bun would be unfashionable on a scullery maid. To distract herself from Sir Frederick's possible motives (the most obvious being a desire to gratify her, of course) Angela began to calculate just what would need to be done to render her sister presentable.

Brie was watching the play, the first she had ever seen, although her complete attention was not claimed. Having read *The Taming of the Shrew* more than once, however, she was not concerned that she would lose the thread of the plot. Sir Frederick had asked to take her driving on the morrow, and it was this which was currently occupying her thoughts. She had not missed the slightly sour look Angela had directed at the pair, and wondered whether she might refuse permission for such an outing.

She hoped not. She was aware of a purely feminine thrill of gratification at Sir Frederick's attentions, which helped her to forget, for the moment, her sister's barbed comments about her appearance. Sir Frederick seemed not to find her dowdy at all! Though, she admitted to herself, that could be simple politeness, for even she realised how *démodé* she was. Thus, her thoughts began to parallel her sister's.

During the drive home, Brie tentatively brought up the subject of Sir Frederick's proposed outing. "May I go, Angela?" she asked hopefully.

Lady Platt had feared something of this nature, but luckily a ready excuse presented itself. "Why, certainly I have no objection to your driving out with Sir Frederick, who is, after all, one of our closest friends" (which stretched the matter slightly, as Sir Frederick and Sir Seymour were barely nodding acquaintances), "but you must agree that your wardrobe must be our first consideration, before you can afford to be seen so publicly."

Brie murmured that she supposed this was so.

"I had thought to spend the greater part of tomorrow at one or two of the better modistes, and perhaps to stop by one of the bookstores on the way home."

As she had expected it would, this last item successfully diverted her younger sister's thoughts.

"A bookstore! I should love that!" she exclaimed. "There is one in particular I wish to look for, as I promised Gabe to try to find it." After a moment's happy consideration of the treat in store, she turned her thoughts back to the original subject. "I suppose you are right, anyway, about the drive. I shouldn't wish to embarrass you by appearing in the Park dressed like this."

"Nor would I wish you embarrassed," said her sister, sounding unexpectedly sincere. "Since that is settled, I shall just send a note round to Sir Frederick first thing in the morning with your excuses." As well as a few pointed remarks on her own behalf, she thought.

"Thank you, Angela. You're being very good to me," said Brie and, to her surprise, she meant it. Perhaps it would be as well if she allowed herself to be guided by her sister, at least in *some* things.

CHAPTER FOUR

"GADSLIFE, DEX, I'm glad to see you back in Town!" exclaimed Lord Garvey, rising from the table at White's where he awaited luncheon. "Will you join me?" He motioned towards the empty chair opposite him.

"It was with that intention that I followed you here," returned his friend with a smile. "I barely missed you at your lodgings, but your man told me I would find you here."

"Yes, Graves is invaluable. Keeps better track of me than I do myself." Lord Garvey brushed back his perpetually askew fair hair with one hand. "So, what news? Were you successful with the beauteous Monique, or do I win the wager?"

"I'm afraid you do, damn your luck, Barry!" Ravenham favoured his companion with a twisted grin; he had not yet fully recovered from that blow to his not inconsiderable pride.

"Luck had nothing to do with it, m'boy!" crowed Garvey. "Told you she was holding out for royalty—not that she'll necessarily get it, mind. Though something I heard night before last about one of the Dukes—"

"Cut the gossip, I beg you," broke in Ravenham hastily. "You've won your wager, but as I recall, you have yet to name the stakes. Couldn't it just be money this time?"

"Too dull, Dex! Can't be getting a reputation for conformity!" said Garvey with the boyish smile which certain ladies had been known to find irresistible. "Tell you what! The next man through the door shall determine your penalty—you'll owe him a favour of his choosing!"

"I only hope it's someone more reasonable than yourself," returned Ravenham, turning towards the door. "Of course, my odds of that are excellent."

A scant minute later a figure entered which caused one of the watching gentlemen to stifle a groan and the other to chuckle quietly. "Of all the accursed luck!" muttered Ravenham. "Why was that nodcock ever allowed in here in the first place?"

"Joined before the bottle claimed him, I believe, though I'll admit he was a nodcock even then," returned Garvey. "Fact remains, though, you owe Sir Seymour Platt a favour of his choosing!"

ANGELA AND GABRIELLA returned to the house from an exhausting day of shopping just before tea to be informed by an obviously curious Madsen that Sir Seymour was closeted in the library with the Duke of Ravenham, and had been so for nearly an hour.

"Did he say what his business was?" enquired Lady Platt, feeling the liveliest curiosity herself.

"No, my lady."

"Was my husband—er—in a condition to receive him?" she then asked almost tentatively. Why the illustrious duke might have called she could not imagine, but it was to be devoutly hoped that he might carry away a good impression. His patronage could mean everything—he was thick as thieves with most of the patronesses of Almack's, for one thing—and his censure could lead to social ostracism, so high was the duke's standing.

"I believe so, madam," returned Madsen, much to her relief. "He had arisen but an hour before, and had not had time to fortify himself with more than a single glass of wine, to the best of my knowledge."

Thus reassured, Angela seemed to suddenly recall her dignity. "Thank you, Madsen. Tell Mrs. Madsen to serve tea in the front drawing room in a quarter of an hour."

"Very good, madam," replied the butler as the ladies mounted the staircase.

"Whatever can he want, I wonder?" At a time like this, Lady Platt found her sister's ear adequate, as a servant's obviously would not do.

Brie, who had gathered from the exchange below that such a visit was very much out of the ordinary, had no theory to offer. "No doubt Sir Seymour will inform us once the duke has departed," was the best she could do.

Angela favoured her with an impatient glance. "You can be sure he will! We had best change for tea immediately. And *do* try to look your best, for the Duke of Ravenham will likely be joining us! As you are new to Town, I suppose I must inform you that the duke is one of the highest sticklers of the ton and must *not* be offended."

"I shall be most careful," said Brie, hoping her sister heard the edge to her voice. She went at once to her room to avoid any further such advice.

When the ladies descended a few minutes later, Brie in a lilac muslin bought just that morning which needed taking in but was more presentable than anything else she owned, Sir Seymour was waiting for them, a satisfied smile upon his dissipated countenance. The duke was not in evidence.

"My dear, you will never guess who was just here" were his first words, uttered in a tone which implied an intention to keep the ladies guessing as long as possible.

"What? Has Ravenham gone already?" was his loving wife's reply. "Never tell me that you neglected to ask him to tea?"

Sir Seymour looked crestfallen that his great secret was no secret after all, but quickly recovered his spirits upon recollecting the good news he would still be able to share with his lady. "Indeed I did invite him, but he would go. However, I have some information to impart over our own tea that I am persuaded you will find *most* agreeable."

This was sufficient to pique even Brie's interest, and Angela was nearly beside herself with curiosity. Without a word, the ladies followed Sir Seymour into the elegantly gaudy parlour and seated themselves.

"Well?" demanded Lady Platt, when her husband showed no immediate sign of unburdening himself. "What is this wonderful news? I don't suppose the duke came to offer for my sister, sight unseen?" she asked sarcastically.

But Sir Seymour was enjoying the rare treat of being in control of a situation and had no mind to give it up so easily. "Not quite that, my dear, but perhaps you are closer to the mark than you realise," he said tantalisingly.

Brie paled slightly at this, but made no comment; Angela was not to be put off, however. "Enough of this tiptoeing about the edges of the issue, Seymour!" she exclaimed. "What did the man want? And pray tell us in plain words."

"Oh, very well, my dear," replied her husband almost regretfully. "In short, it was a matter of a wager."

"What?" Lady Platt fairly shrieked. "Never say you have lost our livelihood to the Duke of Ravenham! You promised not to wager beyond the monthly amount I set for you, and you could never be such a fool as to think you could best someone like him! Why, the man's luck is legendary!"

"Not this time, apparently," returned Sir Seymour, still smug. "No, my dear," he said to his wife's suddenly hopeful glance, "I did not game with him, but I still seem to have come out the winner." Both ladies gazed at him in perplexity. "Lord Garvey, with his odd wagers, appears to be our benefactor. He and Ravenham wagered over some matter, the details of which I was not told—" he pursed his thin lips over this omission "—and the duke lost. Garvey insisted that he do a favour for the next man to enter White's, and that lucky fellow happened to be myself!"

Now Angela's eyes fairly glowed. "A favour, from the Duke of Ravenham! Why, it is in his power to restore me— us—to the very pinnacle of Society! Almack's! You must tell him to speak to Lady Jersey to have our vouchers restored—"

But Sir Seymour was speaking again. "It is already settled, my dear, and I flatter myself that I managed to hit on the very thing. The duke has agreed to help us fire off little Gabriella in style—establish her in the forefront of Society. That way she will have the best possible chance of marrying advantageously. There! Did I not do well?" Sir Seymour sat back, awaiting his wife's praise.

"You...he...when I could have..." Incoherent as this speech was, it nevertheless conveyed to her listeners that Lady Platt was less than overjoyed. Brie had no trouble understanding this, but her brother-in-law was perplexed.

"But my angel!" he exclaimed anxiously. "Is this not exactly what you wished for your sister? You have said time and again that if only she might marry a man of fortune you should never have to listen to your mother's importunings again."

Angela quelled him with a glance; it did not suit her to have her motives so openly discussed. "That was not what I said, and you know it, Seymour." He did not dare to contradict her. "I only meant that it would please my mother prodigiously to see Gabriella well settled, which is perfectly true. Is it not, my dear?" she asked, turning to her sister.

Brie nodded mutely. It would not please *her* prodigiously, but she saw no particular point in saying so at this juncture.

By now, Angela had had time to consider all the ramifications of the duke's "favour" and was beginning to see various ways of turning it to her own advantage. After all, Gabriella could hardly attend any social functions (or even Almack's) alone, and what more obvious chaperone could there be than her loving sister, who had brought her to Town in the first place? If she played her cards right, she herself could be reestablished at the pinnacle of Society along with her drab little sister. And who could tell? Perhaps Gabriella really could manage a respectable match with Ravenham's patronage, and Lady Platt could take a large part of the credit.

With a sudden, blinding smile at Brie, she said, "But of course you did the right thing, Seymour! I was merely overcome by surprise at first. This will be the very thing for Gabriella. When does the duke propose to start this, ah, project?"

"He said he would call upon us in two days' time, to meet Gabriella and to discuss the particulars—that means who's going to come up with the ready, I expect."

"Pray try to refrain from vulgarity, Seymour," said Angela absently. She was thinking hard. "Two days. We'd best get an early start again tomorrow, Gabriella. We have a great deal to accomplish in that time."

BRIE HAD THOUGHT that first day of shopping with her sister was gruelling, but it was as nothing compared to the second. Not that it involved much in the way of physical exertion—that she was well used to and could have managed—but the tediousness of shop after shop, measuring after measuring, with all decisions taken out of her hands, took its toll on her. To be sure, some lovely fabrics had been purchased, to be worked into very fetching gowns, if the drawings shown her by the modistes were to be believed, but she couldn't help but wonder if they could possibly be worth the effort—and expense!

The first real conflict between the sisters occurred late on that second day, when Lady Platt introduced Brie to her personal hairdresser, Monsieur Philippe, with the announcement that he was to cut Miss Gordon's mane to a fashionable length. Miss Gordon adamantly refused.

"But Gabriella, dear, you must know that no one is now wearing hair so long as yours! It went out of fashion quite five years ago, and even then very few were to be seen thus." Angela's tone was that of a reasonable adult trying to persuade a sulky child, which was less than conciliatory.

"I'm sorry, Angela," said Brie firmly. "Your *monsieur* may style my hair in any way you or he sees fit, but it shall not be cut. Papa told me many times that he loved it long, and I feel that it would be disrespectful to his memory to cut it."

To Brie's surprise and Angela's disgust, Monsieur Philippe agreed instantly, with all the fervour of a Frenchman. "But of course, *mademoiselle*, with such a reason as this we must not shear you of your memories. So fine a thing, to honour the memory of one's papa! Come, be seated, and I shall see what I may do with these glorious tresses." He let them fall through the fingers of one hand, considering. "Perhaps if I may thin it a bit? But to leave the length as it is, I assure you!"

Brie agreed, somewhat uncertainly. The man definitely seemed understanding enough.

"But Monsieur Philippe, the pictures I showed you..." began Lady Platt indignantly, to be waved to silence by the artist as he contemplated.

"*Non, madame,*" he said loftily. "I am the last man you would find to dishonour the dead. Perhaps you would leave us a moment while I create." With a strangled exclamation of outrage, Lady Platt flounced out of the chamber, pointedly leaving the door open. Scarcely noticing her exit, Monsieur Philippe returned to the task at hand.

A scant hour later, Brie had been transformed. The majority of her hair had been gathered up on top of her head in an intricate knot which left the ends to curl about her shoulders. She had consented to have a few wisps about her face cut short and they now formed carefully careless ringlets which framed it charmingly. She gazed into the mirror finally handed her by the hairdresser with admiring disbelief. How could a mere hairstyle effect such a transformation? She felt as she looked: elegant, dainty, ladylike. It was an unfamiliar feeling, but she found that she liked it.

Her sister strode in a moment later, and the surprise which wiped away her aggrieved expression was comic. She opened and closed her mouth several times before saying, "Monsieur Philippe, I believe you must be a magician! Who would have believed it? Gabriella, little as I like to say it, your stubbornness may have served you a good turn in this instance. I dare swear you shall start a new fashion, once Ravenham is seen to notice you." She was quite as startled as her sister had been at the change the new hairstyle had wrought, though perhaps a shade less pleased.

THE NEXT DAY, precisely at four, as he had agreed to come for tea, the Duke of Ravenham was announced.

Brie was clad, for once, in a gown which actually fit, through the exertions of Lady Platt, who had alternately bullied and bribed the dressmaker. The day dress was charmingly constructed, with several flounces at the hem, but the colour was an insipid yellow which did nothing for her complexion. Brie couldn't help wondering if this was intentional on the part of her sister, as she herself was wearing an outrageously low-cut gown of vivid blue, making the contrast between them nearly as striking as it had been on Brie's first day in London. She could not bring herself to voice such a suspicion, however, for the vast (to her) amounts of money her sister had lately expended on her behalf had engendered both awe and gratitude.

All such speculation was abruptly cut off by the entrance of the gentleman they awaited with varying degrees of eagerness. The past two days had given Brie ample opportunity to picture to herself the probable appearance of her benefactor. He would be a distinguished-looking man of middle age, possibly with a strong reputation in politics, who would publicly treat her as a niece or some other connection, thus assuring the world of her respectability. A paragon himself, he might even drop a hint to the other paragons of Society that Miss Gabriella Gordon would be an asset at any of their gatherings. She had not thought to verify these surmises with her sister, and thus was herself partially responsible for the shock she now sustained.

Looking up as he was announced, Brie felt the polite smile she had donned for the occasion stiffen as she froze in disbelief. The Duke of Ravenham was none other than the arrogant nobleman she had crossed swords with at the Ruby Crown!

CHAPTER FIVE

As THE INTRODUCTIONS were made, it first appeared that Ravenham did not recognise Brie from their previous encounter. His glance slid negligently past her and Sir Seymour, coming to rest on the opulent charms of her sister, so vividly displayed. Brie was unsure whether the slight lift of his brows at the sight denoted amusement or distaste; it certainly did not appear to be the admiration Lady Platt so obviously expected.

The duke's entire demeanour upon entering implied a strong desire on his part to be anywhere else, and Brie's discomfort increased. Of course, the man was here as the result of a lost wager and not by his own inclination, she reminded herself. But did he have to make it so obvious?

"And this is my wife's sister, Miss Gabriella Gordon, whom you have agreed to sponsor, Your Grace," Sir Seymour was saying. Brie murmured an acknowledgement of the introduction, determined to betray no recognition if the duke did not. However, at the sound of her voice, he swung his gaze away from Lady Platt's cleavage and fixed it on Miss Gordon's face in a disbelief which matched her own of a moment before.

"Your servant, Miss Gordon," said Ravenham before his silence could be considered rude. That low, musical voice, those unusual turquoise eyes—surely he could not be mistaken? Could there be two such girls in England? But the dress, the hair...surely this could not be the serving wench who had so boldly accosted him at the Ruby Crown! More likely a chance resemblance, he finally decided.

So, thought Brie, *he recognises me but chooses not to acknowledge it. Very well, I shall play along—for now.* She felt her composure returning as the memory of the anger she had felt at the duke's treatment of his horse—and of herself—came to her aid. She might just have a chance to bring him to a better understanding of his responsibilities, after all!

"Perhaps you would care to pour out for us, Gabriella," said Lady Platt smoothly, seating herself and gesturing Ravenham to the chair next to her. Her tone was condescending, and Brie seethed inwardly that her sister would treat her so in front of their guest. She gave no hint of her feelings to the others, however, but proceeded to obey what had been little short of an order. His Grace, she noticed, ignored the indicated chair and placed himself at her own side instead; while not actually desiring his attention, she could not suppress a small surge of satisfaction at Angela's barely concealed discomfiture.

"Yes, this is the young lady we spoke of, Ravenham," drawled Sir Seymour into the silence, apparently feeling it high time they got down to business. "Still think you can pull it off?"

Brie squirmed at her brother-in-law's vulgar insensitivity, and even Ravenham had the grace to look embarrassed at such plain speaking, but he answered readily enough.

"I foresee no difficulty whatever. I must say you hardly did your sister-in-law justice in your description; she is even lovelier than you led me to believe." This last was said gallantly, and almost as an afterthought, as though he had suddenly realised what the first part of his sentence had implied.

For her part, Brie could well imagine the unflattering picture which Sir Seymour, ever guided by his lady's judgement, had undoubtedly painted. The thought did not trouble her unduly, but she almost grudgingly appreciated the duke's tactful handling of the situation. Looking side-long at his handsome, masculine profile, such a stark contrast to Sir Seymour's effete one, she wondered if it were vaguely possible that she might have misjudged him. Her thoughts went involuntarily back to their confronta-tion at the inn, and she uncomfortably wondered what his wife's opinion of this bargain might be.

"Am I to understand that you are but lately come to Town, Miss Gordon?" asked Ravenham, cutting off whatever Sir Seymour had been about to say.

"Yes, I have been here but three days, Your Grace," she replied, not meeting his eyes. Suddenly, unaccountably, she felt shy of him and assiduously stirred her tea, almost hoping that he had not recognised her, after all.

"So you can well understand, Your Grace, that we have had little time to outfit my dear sister fashionably," broke in Lady Platt at this juncture, refusing to be ignored any longer. "The gowns she brought with her were simply decades out of mode, so it may be a few days yet before she will be ready to go out in public much. Only a few things have been purchased so far."

"If this is an example," said Ravenham, his gesture taking in the yellow muslin Brie wore, "I can hardly fault the style, though the colour might have been better cho-sen."

Brie barely managed to conceal a chuckle, while Lady Platt's bosom swelled with silent indignation, as this gown, along with the other recent purchases, had been her own choice. Before she could swell completely out of the top of her bodice, as Brie was beginning to fear she might, she managed to control her resentment, realising that she could scarcely afford to queer the game so early.

"What colours would you deem more appropriate, Your Grace?" she managed to ask sweetly after a brief but ruthless battle with her feelings.

The duke turned to examine the girl beside him with a thoroughness which caused her to colour slightly. "Blues, I think," he replied at length, "but not the pale insipid ones you see on so many debutantes. Her colouring demands richer shades, perhaps of aqua, to match her eyes. Deep rose should look well on her also, and . . . have you ordered her a habit yet?"

Angela shook her head. "There hasn't been time . . ."

"A golden brown velvet would be just the thing," he said decisively, not waiting for her reasons. "Perhaps a hat to match. Her hair . . ."

"I *tried* to have it cut, Your Grace, I assure you, but she would have none of it, I fear. Some sentimental rubbish about our father. Perhaps your word will carry more weight than mine in the matter."

"I was going to say that such a habit as I suggested should set off her hair to advantage. I believe we should consider her hair quite an asset, as a matter of fact, and under no circumstances should it be cut."

Lady Platt was chagrined. "But the fashion, Your Grace," she began uncertainly, but he shook his head.

"Short hair has been the fashion these three years and more, and I predict that to change no later than next season. Already the styles are longer in Paris, and you know what that means." Lady Platt nodded vigorously. "Far better to be ahead of the styles than behind them, you must agree."

Brie was beginning to tire of the way she was being discussed as though she were not present. A portrait of her would have done quite as well as her actual presence, she thought with some irritation. Before she could say something of the sort, however, the duke turned to her again, and she was forced to catch her breath at the impact of the smile he suddenly bestowed on her.

"There, Miss Gordon, we must not forget your feelings in this," he said, as if he could read her mind. "If you would care to ride out with me tomorrow, we can discuss these things further as well as begin our campaign to take London by storm. Would that be convenient?"

She nodded wordlessly, the intensity of his grey eyes having a disturbing effect on her pulse. *Had* he recognised her? Now she wasn't so sure.

"That would be splendid, Your Grace," Angela answered for her. "Is it too much to hope that you could see your way clear to obtain the entrée to Almack's for my sister?" she asked, keeping her own ends well in view.

"I already have the matter in hand, my lady, I assure you," he replied, suddenly bored. "And now, I must take my leave, I fear. I am expected at White's."

Brie tried to ignore the obsequious manners of her brother-in-law and, to a lesser extent, of her sister as they bade the Duke farewell, with many protestations of gratitude for something he was clearly doing against his will. Embarrassed, she tried to compensate by taking leave of him as quietly and composedly as was possible without actual coldness. As her eyes were downcast, she missed the look of approval he cast at her before he turned to go.

"Almack's!" exclaimed Lady Platt, almost before the front door had closed behind him. "'Tis too good to be true, I declare! You did very well after all, Seymour!" She was in charity with all the world at that moment. "If

Ravenham requests vouchers for us, Lady Jersey will never let that little misunderstanding we had stand in the way. Why just everyone knows she positively dotes on him! Almack's," she concluded dreamily.

Turning to Brie, she continued in a more businesslike manner. "First thing tomorrow we must order you that brown velvet riding habit which the Duke recommended. His taste is absolutely impeccable, you know; we must let him guide us as far as possible in matters of dress." Brie doubted that this would apply to Lady Platt's dress, of which His Grace obviously disapproved. "Perhaps I can change some of the gowns we have already ordered to blue and rose. Madsen! Bring me paper and pen and send for a footman at once." She engaged herself with writing notes to the dressmakers, and Brie was finally able to slip up to her room to think.

Settling herself upon the chaise among the soothing blues of her bedchamber, Brie carefully reviewed the duke's visit. On reflection, she was not at all certain that he had recognised her as the shabby girl who had berated him at the Ruby Crown four days earlier. She had changed quite a bit since then, she had to admit. And so had he. Oh, he was as handsome as ever, with his powerful build, curling chestnut hair and cool grey eyes—which had warmed once or twice today. That was just it. He hadn't resembled the cold, arrogant beast at the inn in the least, and she did not know what to make of that.

Remembering the inn, a vision of the duke's poor mistreated horse jumped unbidden to her mind. Could the man she had met today be capable of such cruelty? It seemed incredible, but she recalled that he had not even attempted to deny her accusations at the time. No doubt he was so affable today simply because he was among people he wished to impress. From what Angela had told

her, the duke held an extremely high position in Society,
and no doubt that position would suffer if his true nature
became known. She smiled to herself. Perhaps here was a
weapon which, properly wielded, could force His Grace to
treat his animals better.

THE NEXT MORNING was another whirlwind of activity
throughout every shop in London, it seemed to Brie, as
Lady Platt sought feverishly to comply with the Duke of
Ravenham's recommendations. Half made up gowns were
disposed of in favour of others of similar style but in hues
more flattering to Miss Gordon's colouring. Now despised were the whites and pastels which had been so im-
periously ordered but two days before; these were
pronounced impossibly passé, and summarily replaced by
the deep roses and rich blues His Grace had decreed.

Brie could not help feeling that all this was entirely friv-
olous, as well as ridiculously expensive. Why, the amount
of money being spent, nay, even that being wasted on the
changes, would feed most of their small Gloucestershire
village for several years!

Even so, she could not bring herself to be displeased
with the new riding habit which was ordered, though it
alone cost more than some horses would. But if anything
was worth the expense, surely this was: a rich, golden
brown velvet that exactly matched her hair, even to its
changing highlights. She knew she would look well in it,
and could scarcely wait for it to be finished. Its comple-
tion would also mean that she could resume riding, which
had always been a large, and beloved, part of her life,
though most had hitherto been in the course of helping
with her father's practice.

Upon leaving the last of the shops, that of the particularly exclusive (and expensive) modiste, Madame Boujais,

the sisters encountered Sir Frederick More. He immediately turned to walk with them, as charming and affable as ever. Lady Platt preened under his compliments and possessively took his arm, though he still managed to bestow a flattering amount of attention on Miss Gordon. Brie found him every bit as pleasant as she had at the theatre and could not but be pleased at his comments about her changed appearance.

"Gadsteeth, 'tis like a miracle, Miss Gordon!" he exclaimed almost at once. "You were pretty enough the other night, but now you have added fashion to your other charms. Once the Season is well under way, I dare swear I shall have to stand in line to so much as speak with you."

She denied this with becoming modesty, replying that no amount of popularity could cause her to forget his kindness on her first evening in London. He took his leave as they reached their carriage, his smile bestowed equally upon the sisters.

"I must warn you against taking Sir Frederick's flattery too much to heart, Gabriella," said Angela abruptly as the coach began to move. "He is very pleasant, to be sure, but it can do you no good to encourage him, nor to be seen too much in his company."

Brie looked at her sister in surprise, for she herself had treated Sir Frederick as a close friend. One look at Angela's discontented face, however, told her that jealousy, rather than concern for propriety, had motivated her speech.

"I was not aware that I was 'encouraging' the gentleman," she replied stiffly, embarrassed that it might have appeared so. "Surely, though, as he is your friend, there can be no harm in my being seen with him?"

"As long as it is in that context, no," said her sister, softening slightly. She did not wish to antagonise Ga-

briella just now, she remembered. "I only advise you to be
cautious. You would not wish to be considered *fast,* you
know."

"Certainly not!" exclaimed Brie, even more embarrassed. "I thank you for the advice, and will endeavour to
abide by it." And she almost meant it.

THAT AFTERNOON, AS PROMISED, the Duke of Ravenham
arrived to take Miss Gordon driving in the Park. Before
she left, Lady Platt drew her aside for a parting admoni-
tion.

"For pity's sake remember to say nothing about our
father's profession! Ravenham is one of the highest sticklers in Town, and would no doubt wash his hands of the
entire bargain if he were to discover that."

Brie was unwise enough to roll her eyes at this repeti-
tion of previous advice, at which her sister hissed, "I mean
it! If you ruin this chance for me, I shall never forgive
you!" At that moment, the duke strolled within earshot,
making a reply impossible, but her sister's final words lingered in Brie's mind as they departed for their drive.

The high-perch phaeton was a new experience for Brie.
Ravenham watched her closely as she took her seat, half
expecting her to squeal or clutch the side as many other
young ladies of his acquaintance had been known to do
when in that precarious position, especially for the first
time. Instead, her eyes sparkled and she looked about her
excitedly. He could not know that part of her attention was
claimed by a close inspection of the matched greys which
drew the phaeton.

"Shall we be off?" he asked as soon as she was settled.
She nodded, watching the paces of the greys without
seeming to. These horses, at least, had obviously been well
cared for, to judge by their sleek coats and smooth gaits.

They drove in silence for some way, Brie enjoying the sight of London from this new vantage point. As they entered the gates of Hyde Park, the duke began to outline some of his plans for her debut. His tone was cool and formal, as though to contradict the warmth she thought she had detected in him yesterday. She tried to listen as he spoke of certain balls and routs that she had to be seen at, but her senses were all but overwhelmed by the scene before her.

Why, half of the fashionable world, and some not so fashionable, must be out driving in the Park at this hour! Not all the horses, she noticed, were as healthy as the duke's; some were little better than broken-down nags. For the most part, though, these were driven or ridden by men who could hardly be considered members of the ton, though that certainly did not excuse them.

"...by the middle of next week," Ravenham was saying. Brie realised with a start that she had completely lost the thread of his conversation—or lecture, to be more precise.

"I beg your pardon, Your Grace?" she asked in some embarrassment. "I fear I was not fully attending."

He raised an eyebrow at this, but merely repeated, "I said that I hope to have your voucher to you by next Wednesday or Thursday. For Almack's, you know."

"Oh! Thank you, Your Grace." She felt that some show of gratitude must certainly be called for here. Angela had thoroughly impressed her with the importance of being seen at that holy of holies, and she knew that her sister would be pleased.

"I will escort you there the following Wednesday, and to Lady Bellerby's ball and one or two other dos. By the end of May, if your brother-in-law agrees, we can consider this matter at an end. You should be quite firmly established by then, I imagine, and should do very well for yourself.'' His tone was cynical, and Brie coloured uncomfortably.

"I wish you to know that I had no part in this whatsoever, Your Grace!'' It seemed imperative that he understand that. "My opinion was not sought before this…agreement was entered upon. If it had been, I would have refused, I assure you!''

"But you do not draw back now, I notice,'' he drawled, the half smile playing about his lips belied by the coolness in his eyes.

"Your Grace, you may consider yourself released from any obligation to me or my family as of this moment!'' she exclaimed hotly, stung by his look. "Pray return me to my sister's house at once!''

"If that is your wish,'' he replied equably, turning the horses. She could not help but notice the strength in his large hands as he effortlessly controlled the ribbons. "We cannot, however, end the agreement yet. I have never been a man to go back on his word, and do not intend to change now. I have not yet paid my losses.''

She favoured him with an eloquently indignant glance at his phrasing but said nothing and they completed their drive in silence. She forbore to invite him inside, though she knew this would vex her sister, and bade him a cool farewell at the door.

BRIE NEXT SAW ANGELA when she and her sister were descending to dinner that evening. Lady Platt was attired in an evening gown of pale pink gauze with gold leaves strewn across the tight-fitting and low-cut bodice, as she and Sir Seymour were to go out after dinner.

Brie was not to accompany them, which suited her completely, as she had managed to obtain two books for

Gabe at one of the booksellers the day before and wished to read them herself before sending them off to him. One was Sir William Moorcroft's treatise on horseshoeing, which she had purchased not so much because she felt that there was more that she or her brother needed to know about the subject as because Sir William had been a contemporary and friend of her father's before Sir William had left England to become a celebrated explorer in India. The other was a general anatomy of the horse, which looked as though it might be very useful.

Upon meeting Brie at the head of the stairs, Lady Platt bombarded her with questions. "How went your ride with Ravenham?" she asked eagerly. "What did he say? What are his plans? Does he mean to squire you about himself, or merely to be seen talking to you?"

"Apparently he intends to escort me to at least two evening functions, as well as to Almack's a fortnight hence," replied Brie, certain that this information would put her sister in the best possible mood. Nor was she disappointed.

"It is true, then, as he said! Did he give you our vouchers today?" Lady Platt's eyes fairly glowed at this triumph. How could she ever have regretted her invitation to this dear little sister?

"No, he said he would send them round next week. He also mentioned Lady Bellerby's ball, I believe, as well as a rout at a countess's house—Levy? Something like that."

"Lieven," breathed Lady Platt, almost reverently. "The Countess Lieven, one of the patronesses at Almack's. My—your—social position is assured, dear Gabriella." They had halted by the double doors to the dining room. "Come, let us tell Seymour the good news!" she exclaimed, as Madsen belatedly opened for them. The butler was surprised and gratified when, instead of the scold

he had expected for his tardiness, his mistress favoured him
with a dazzling smile.

The Platts could talk of nothing else during dinner, Sir
Seymour congratulating himself on his own good sense
and quick thinking three days prior and his lady chatter-
ing excitedly of the social triumphs she confidently expected. There was even some talk of giving a ball herself
for her sister's come-out, something she would not have
dared to consider a few days earlier, for fear of being
snubbed by the more highly exalted.

"Perhaps by the fourth week of the Season," she mused
aloud. "We shall just see how things develop. Who knows?
By then it may even be an occasion to announce your engagement, Gabriella!"

Brie quickly changed the subject with a question she had
been meaning to ask. "I was wondering, Angela, whether
I will meet the Duchess of Ravenham at one of these
events, or whether I should perhaps call on her first. I wish
you would advise me in what would be proper."

"The duchess?" asked Angela, obviously perplexed.
"Ravenham's mother? She died before his father did, I
believe. Perhaps it is his sister you mean, the Lady Elizabeth. I believe she is still abroad but, even were she in
Town, I am afraid it might be thought presumptuous if
you were to call on her. After all, it is not as though
Ravenham is doing this out of the kindness of his heart."

Lady Platt resumed planning for her hypothetical ball,
but Brie was not attending. Her thoughts were completely
taken up by what she had just heard. So there was no
duchess! Her feelings vacillated between embarrassment at
the implications of the scene she had witnessed at the Ruby
Crown and a definite sense of relief. But why should she
feel relief? she asked herself. This only went to prove that

the Duke of Ravenham was as immoral as he was cruel. So telling herself, she gave her attention to the sweetmeats being served and resolved to put the man out of her thoughts entirely—at least until the next time they met.

CHAPTER SIX

"No, Barry, I can unequivocally say that neither Sir Seymour nor his wife improve in the least upon closer acquaintance. Rather the opposite, in fact."

The Duke of Ravenham was lounging at his ease in the study of his own town house, with his friend sitting across from him and one of his famous hunting hounds curled up at his feet. He seemed entirely unconcerned that the damp nose resting on his right boot might dull its dazzling shine; it was well known to his intimates that his dogs were the one thing which took precedence over fashion with the fastidious duke.

"Not even Lady Platt, eh?" returned Lord Garvey sympathetically. "I seem to recall her as a taking little thing when she first came to Town—was it five years ago?—as a new bride. Haven't seen her about as much lately, though."

"Having been subjected to her version of the social graces, I'm not surprised. She's bold as brass, and not very polished brass, either, for all she is still *physically* attractive enough. I daresay she has offended more than one of the higher sticklers."

"Yourself, for one," stated Garvey, surveying his companion's expression of distaste. "But what of the sister? Is she the drab country bumpkin Sir Seymour described, or a younger version of her lovely but tasteless elder sibling?"

"Neither, I would say," replied Ravenham thoughtfully. "In fact, I can detect no family resemblance whatsoever, which is all to the good, in my opinion."

"Speaking of the family, I suppose that *is* all right? No tradesmen in the background or anything of that sort?"

"No, no, I did a bit of research there. Father the second son of a viscount, mother granddaughter to the fourth Earl of Wyndover. Only thing a bit off is that the father was a veterinary surgeon, but that's perfectly respectable—not as though he were a blacksmith, after all. Besides, he's dead, so his profession is hardly likely to become common knowledge." He decided against confiding the date of that gentleman's death.

"Your campaign sounds quite hopeful, then. If she were completely *outré*, I would have to consider your debt paid with an honest attempt at establishing her. As it is, perhaps the girl should have to contract a respectable marriage for full payment!"

"Not in the bargain, Barry! However, I think I shall have a fairly easy time getting her to take, if I can successfully keep her relatives out of the way. I hear that Lady Platt is no longer welcome at Almack's, so that problem is already disposed of."

"Who will act the chaperone, then? Elizabeth?" Garvey's tone was careless.

"Of course. She's back in Town now, after finishing at that seminary and spending the past year or so with Aunt Charlotte in Paris. She hasn't had much of a chance to meet anyone as yet, and should enjoy the companionship."

"This Miss Gordon must be to your liking if you're willing to have her intimate with your sister," conjectured Garvey, blatantly probing for more details.

"So far," replied Ravenham, with a look that told his friend he was perfectly aware of what he was about. "Still, she *is* Lady Platt's sister, and will bear watching. Already she has not been as honest with me as I could wish."

"Oh?" Garvey was alert. "What has she done?"

"It's what she hasn't done—or said." He briefly recounted the meeting at the Ruby Crown, and had Garvey howling with laughter at the end of it.

"You, of all people!" he gasped. "To have *that* laid at your door! But if she was dressed as a serving wench, as you say, it's no wonder if she's hoping you haven't recognised her. Just trying for a clean slate, I should say. Nothing particularly dishonest in that—not as women go."

"I suppose you're right, Barry. I shall give her the benefit of the doubt, for the present at least. I'll still keep my eyes open, though."

"One always should," returned his friend philosophically. "Now, about that luncheon I was promised?"

THE DAY AFTER this conversation took place, a breathlessly awaited event occurred at the Platt household, but not with the anticipated results. The envelope containing Miss Gordon's voucher for Almack's arrived, but it resided in the envelope alone. Lady Platt's outrage defied description, and the brunt of her anger fell upon her sister's head, there being no other convenient target at hand.

"You conniving little snake in the grass!" was one of the first epithets used. "You planned this with Ravenham, just to mortify me, to pay me back for some imagined slight. When I have done so much for you! Have you any idea how much I've spent on your wardrobe? On dancing lessons? And to think of the time I have wasted telling you how to go on in Society!"

She continued in this vein for some time. Brie found it worse than useless to try to defend herself against the torrent of abuse, as any word on her part was seen as an added insult, so she silently smoothed the folds of her plum walking dress while awaiting the end of Angela's tirade. Finally running out of words or breath, Lady Platt sent her to her room to meditate upon the sins of ingratitude and deceit.

In the comparative haven of her bedchamber, Brie attempted to unravel the puzzle of the single voucher. She had gathered that the duke did not care for the Platts, but this seemed to be no more than petty spite, though why she should have thought him above that she was not certain. But had he not told her that he would be sending vouchers for all of them?

She thought back over their drive together, trying to recall his exact words. Well, perhaps he had not *specifically* said that he would be sending three vouchers, but it had certainly been implied! Surely he must realise what an intolerable position he was putting her in by so blatantly snubbing the relatives she was dependent upon. Perhaps it was a mistake! But no, the note enclosed had said that he would call for Miss Gordon Wednesday next to escort her to Almack's. No mention of the Platts had been made.

Secretly, Brie could not but be relieved that her sister and brother-in-law would not be attending, for she had already observed that their manners appeared little short of ill-bred in comparison to the few other members of the ton she had met; but she was ashamed of that relief. Angela's enumeration of the expenses she had undertaken on her behalf had only underscored her previous feeling of obligation, and she felt that she was turning out to be a very poor sort of guest.

To assuage her own conflicting feelings of relief and guilt, Brie concentrated on the Duke of Ravenham's culpability in this matter and added it to her account of grievances against him. Obviously, her very first impression of him had been correct: he was the most selfish, pompous, insensitive man that had ever lived, not to mention cruel! Perhaps she would tell him so—again—the next time she saw him.

But wait! Was she likely to see him again? As angry as Angela had been, it seemed more than likely that she would be sent back home to Gloucestershire the first thing in the morning. Oddly, the thought was not as comforting as she expected it to be. After all, wasn't she only here to please her mother, counting off the time until she could return to her beloved Cotswold hills? Finally, Brie fell asleep, her dreams a curious mix of rolling hills and London faces.

WHEN BRIE tentatively entered the breakfast parlour the next morning, she was astonished to find a smiling Angela awaiting her, apparently willing to pretend that nothing untoward had happened. She was curious about the cause of this sudden reversal, but too relieved at the cessation of hostilities to risk their renewal by injudicious questioning.

Lady Platt had spent the first hour after sending her sister upstairs the previous night plotting suitable punishments for the girl's perfidy. As her anger cooled, however, she began to realise that there could be little long-term benefit to herself in such a course—only momentary gratification. Gabriella still represented her best chance of regaining her former high place in Society, though perhaps a bit more patience would now be required. Once the girl had taken—as she surely would, with Ravenham's patronage—there would be ample opportunity for her to repay the Platts for their generosity. Also, it was inevitable that invitations would be issued which would include them. Yes, she could afford to bide her time.

It also began to seem less likely that Gabriella had actually planned the insult herself. What influence could a stupid, countrified girl like her sister possibly have with the Duke of Ravenham, after all? It was far more likely that Lady Jersey's unreasonable dislike of herself had proved too immovable for even his best efforts on her behalf.

The idea of the duke exerting himself for her benefit, even if those exertions had proven unavailing, had further cooled her temper. Supremely confident of her influence over men, she did not doubt that he had been as taken with her as every other gentleman of her acquaintance. That he did not display his admiration by any vulgar flattery was merely evidence of his superior breeding.

Thus, it was with the intention of conciliating her sister over the breakfast table that Angela greeted her that morning. Swallowing her own repugnance for the exercise, she even suggested a ride in the Park later that morning.

"Oh, Angela, could we?" exclaimed Brie, sincerely delighted. "I knew you didn't care for riding, so I didn't like to ask, but I've been simply dying to sit a horse again."

Angela forced the smile to remain on her face. "But of course, darling. I knew you would want to try out your new habit, and I have one as well which I have yet to wear, though I have had it these three months. Sir Seymour was saying just last night that there is a gelding in the stables which he thought would be suitable for you."

Sir Seymour had said no such thing, being in no case for any sort of conversation the evening before, but Angela did not want her tactics to appear *too* obvious. She had

questioned the groom about the horses herself that very
morning, remembering that riding had been one of her
sister's favourite pastimes.

They donned their habits after breakfast, therefore, and
met on the front steps, where the saddled horses were being held ready for them. Surveying their mounts, Brie was
torn between amusement and dismay—amusement that
these animals, obviously bred as work horses, should be
kept for riding, and dismay at their condition.

Both were dispirited beasts, showing almost no interest
in their surroundings. The black-and-white gelding, which
she assumed was to be her mount, at least had a slight arch
to his neck. However, the dappled grey mare, almost a
large pony, was so fat that Brie privately doubted she could
achieve a trot. While neither showed signs of outright
abuse, their lackluster coats and dull eyes revealed that the
quality, at least, of their diet was poor and that they had
not had the benefit of regular exercise. Brie considered
taking her sister to task for this neglect but forbore doing
so, in the interests of peace.

The ladies mounted with the groom's assistance, Angela's pride being sufficient to prevent her displaying, even
to her sister and a servant, her fear of the horses. Once up,
they started at a sedate walk (or waddle, in the case of the
mare) for the Park. Brie longed to trot, but one look at her
sister's strained expression told her that it would be worse
than useless to suggest it. Perhaps it might be managed
once they reached the Park, she thought without much
hope.

It took them quite fifteen minutes to cover the quarter
mile to the Park entrance, but Brie was endeavouring to
enjoy this first ride in London in spite of the knowledge
that she would set a quicker pace afoot. With very little
imagination, she could almost make herself believe that

she was back on old Traveller, the pony she had ridden as a child. The thought brought a half smile to her lips just as she looked up into the amused eyes of Sir Frederick, who appeared to be waiting for them at the gates.

Sitting astride a coal black stallion, he looked even more dashing and elegant than she remembered him. Angela seemed to come suddenly to life as they reached him, sitting up straighter in the saddle and shaking back her blonde curls to favour him with her most bewitching smile.

"Sir Frederick, i'faith!" she exclaimed with a little laugh. "I vow you have been almost a stranger this week past! What has been keeping you from us?" Brie quickly coughed to cover the chuckle she had almost emitted at the way her sister was batting her lashes.

"'Twas business of the most tedious sort, my lady, and I will not bore you with the details," replied Sir Frederick, kissing the dimpled hand Lady Platt had extended to him. "Suffice to say I am vastly relieved it is concluded, that I may feast my eyes upon you again."

Brie thought that he was doing it rather brown, but then saw that Angela was positively eating up his fulsome flattery. This was obviously the sort of thing her sister thrived on, and just as obviously, Sir Frederick knew it.

Becoming aware of her regard, Sir Frederick turned towards her. "Miss Gordon! Permit me to say that your habit is charming. It just matches your hair."

She refrained from telling him that the fabric had been chosen with that in mind and thanked him prettily for the compliment. "Would you care to join us on our ride?" she asked, certain that her sister would not object, and hoping that his presence might improve her chances for a trot. She was fairly certain that the nag she rode could not manage anything faster.

He agreed with alacrity and turned his mount, holding the spirited animal to their pace with some little difficulty. He managed to divide his time fairly evenly between the sisters, contriving to further his acquaintance with Miss Gordon without irritating her sister. His original intent in befriending her had merely been to provoke Lady Platt to jealousy, hoping thereby to overcome that lady's reluctance to dally with him. Now, however, he was discovering in the younger sister charms of her own and had begun to revise his plans.

Therefore, still with no definite idea himself of what his true intentions were, Sir Frederick ingratiated himself with both ladies, using for each the type of flattery best suited to their individual personalities. Finally, noticing Miss Gordon subtly urging her mount to walk faster, he asked the sisters if they would care to trot.

"It is perfectly acceptable, you know," he said for Miss Gordon's benefit. "One may even canter in the Park. Only galloping is expressly forbidden."

Brie laughed merrily. "I rather doubt whether this poor fellow could achieve a canter, and I am certain that a gallop would be beyond him, but I would dearly love to trot."

Lady Platt had motioned to her groom and held a quick conference with him. "James wishes to check my mare's feet before I try trotting her. He fears she may have picked up a stone. You two go on ahead, and I will join you in a moment, if all is well." She proceeded to dismount, and Sir Frederick looked enquiringly at his companion.

"Shall we?" He showed no sign that he suspected Lady Platt's ruse, and Brie concluded that he must not be aware of her sister's aversion to riding—and especially to risking her pretty neck by moving any faster than a slow walk.

"Let's," she replied happily, delighted with this chance, and they urged their horses into a trot.

Brie had been right in her suspicions, in that it took quite
a bit of urging to get the gelding to break into a trot, but
once he was going, his gait was fairly smooth and she
found herself enjoying it. Heartened at this success, she
tried for more speed and was pleased to discover that he
was after all capable of a canter, albeit a slow one. Mindful of Sir Frederick's words, and the gelding's capabilities
(or lack thereof), she did not attempt to spur her mount
any faster.

Sir Frederick kept pace with her, occasionally giving her
an admiring glance, which she could not help but find
gratifying. His solicitude was especially welcome after
yesterday's unpleasantness, and she found herself comparing him—mostly favourably—with the Duke of
Ravenham. To be sure, he was not quite as handsome, but
neither was he arrogant or overbearing. When he looked
at her it was to admire, not to criticise. She found herself
wishing that she were better mounted, that she might appear more to advantage.

As if he read her thoughts, Sir Frederick's first words
when they slowed again to a trot were "You are quite a
horsewoman, Miss Gordon, and it is obvious that your
mount does not do you justice. I am not sure if I could
have got a canter out of him myself. Would you permit me
to mount you on something better?"

Unsure precisely what he meant, she said uncertainly, "I
suppose so, but how?" Surely he did not intend exchanging horses for the rest of the morning!

"I'll call tomorrow morning and you'll see," he said
enigmatically.

They were just completing their circuit of the Park, and
Lady Platt was awaiting them, mounted again on the
mare, so Brie forbore to question him further.

"Her foot was fine," called Lady Platt as they approached. "Poor James must have been seeing things." She frowned at the groom. "By the time he was satisfied that she was all right, it was too late to catch you up."

"We can take another turn, if you wish, my lady," offered Sir Frederick gallantly, but she shook her head prettily.

"I wish I could oblige you, but Gabriella and I must head for home. Shall we see you there soon, Sir Frederick?" Her glance was coquettish.

"I have already told Miss Gordon that I intend to call tomorrow. I shall bid you farewell until then." He sketched a bow from the saddle towards both ladies and rode off, leaving them to return to South Audley Street at Angela's preferred snail's pace.

CHAPTER SEVEN

THE NEXT MORNING Sir Frederick made good his promise, arriving less than fifteen minutes after the sisters had finished breakfasting. Cordial relations still prevailed between Brie and Angela, and they were conversing pleasantly in the parlour when their caller was announced.

"Good morning, ladies," he said, entering briskly. "You are both lovely, as always. But what is this? Neither of you is dressed for riding." Seeing that both ladies looked perplexed, he added, "Surely, Miss Gordon, you told your sister of my promise to mount you. I have brought a mare for your inspection, and if you like the way she goes, she is yours."

"Mine?" gasped Brie in confusion. "Whatever do you mean?" Her sister, she noticed, was regarding her with suspicion.

"I thought it was agreed yesterday. I offered to mount you on something better, if you recall, and..."

"But I thought you only meant to lend me a horse!" she exclaimed, taken aback that she could have been so misunderstood. "You must know I cannot accept such a gift from you, sir!"

"Certainly not, Frederick," interposed Lady Platt. "What can you be thinking of? Gabriella is not one of your high flyers, which is what would undoubtedly be thought if the gift were to become known. Besides, there was nothing wrong with the horse she rode yesterday."

"Now there, I fancy, your sister will disagree with you. I had not realised until yesterday what a poor judge of horseflesh Sir Seymour is. But I assure you, Miss Gordon, I had no intention to offend." His manner was once more kindness itself. "I fear I did not think. I shall merely lend you the mare, of course. But rest assured that you may have the use of her for as long as you wish."

Brie then thanked him warmly, allowing her momentary indignation to be soothed by his apology. Angela gave her permission for the outing, pleading much unattended correspondence as her excuse to bide at home, and Brie went upstairs to change into her habit.

"What game are you playing at, Frederick?" demanded Lady Platt as soon as Brie was out of earshot. "You knew full well, even if she didn't, that it would not be proper for you to gift her with a horse."

"I could not bear to see your little sister dissatisfied with her mount, my dear, that is all," he said soothingly. "I must confess that in my eagerness to please her, and thereby yourself, I did not stop to consider the proprieties."

She regarded him narrowly, but finally nodded. "Very well, Frederick, I forgive you, but pray try to think before you act next time. There are other ways of pleasing me." She lowered her lashes and glanced sideways at him.

He cocked an eyebrow. "Ah, well I know it, if you would only give me the chance!" She lightly tapped his knuckles with her fan as punishment for this satisfactory speech, which assured her that she still came first in his affections.

BRIE FOUND the clean-limbed chestnut mare far superior to the horse she had ridden the day before, and she enjoyed herself immensely—at first. Gradually, however, there was a subtle change in Sir Frederick's manner towards her that was both exciting and alarming. Before, she had always assumed that he was being kind to her because of his long friendship with her sister but today, once they were away from the house and Angela's watchful eye, his attentions became more pronounced than simple kindness would account for.

"I'm not surprised Lady Platt never brought you to Town before this," he said warmly as they turned into the Park gates. "No doubt she feared her little sister would cast her in the shade." He regarded her appreciatively.

"Surely you jest, sir," returned Brie, more seriously than flirtatiously. "I have no illusions about myself, and would thank you not to create any."

His smile broadened. "A treasure indeed! Shall we canter?"

Brie agreed with relief, for she somehow found Sir Frederick's flattery unsettling. She had no trouble urging this mount to greater speed, and was sorely tempted to try a gallop, but refrained. As they finally drew to a stop after nearly half an hour, Sir Frederick complimented her again on her skill.

"I was glad to see that you remembered my warning, for I could see you would have liked to test the mare's limits."

"Yes, she is wonderful!" Brie was still exhilarated from her ride. "What is her name, by the way?"

"I leave that for you to decide," replied Sir Frederick gallantly, but Brie frowned. This came too close to gifting her with the horse, after all.

"Surely she had a name when you purchased her?"

"I believe she was called Bessie, or Bonny or some such common name, but I am certain that you could do better."

Brie bent to pat the mare's neck. "Thank you for a lovely ride, Bessie," she said firmly.

Sir Frederick raised an amused eyebrow but said nothing. They walked their horses in silence for several minutes, the groom slowly falling back at a silent signal from his master.

"Shall we dismount and walk for a bit, Miss Gordon?" he asked presently. She glanced at him, and though his expression seemed innocent enough, somehow Brie felt that it would be unwise to comply.

"No, thank you," she replied in a politely regretful tone. "I really should be getting back. My sister had planned to take me shopping before nuncheon, I believe."

"As you wish, of course," responded Sir Frederick affably. "I only wished to show you a particularly charming garden just the other side of this copse, which artists have been known to admire. Are you certain you would rather not?"

It seemed churlish now to refuse, but Brie realised uncomfortably that they were in a particularly secluded area of the Park and that the groom, suddenly, was nowhere in sight. She was wondering how to diplomatically decline when a voice spoke from behind them.

"Good morning, Miss Gordon, Sir Frederick," drawled the Duke of Ravenham. "Might I accompany you on your ride?" His tone was careless, but when Brie swung round to face him, with something resembling a gasp of relief, she noticed a hardness in his eyes that belied his smile. He was as handsome as ever this morning, astride a roan stallion which dwarfed Sir Frederick's black.

"Thank you, Your Grace, but I was just about to return home," she said somewhat breathlessly, glancing over at Sir Frederick. She thought that he seemed displeased to see the duke, but he spoke civilly enough.

"Yes, Ravenham, we have concluded our ride, and I was about to escort Miss Gordon back to her sister's house." As a dismissal, this speech fell short of its object.

"I had thought to escort her myself, Sir Frederick," replied Ravenham, his tone still pleasant. "You have had the pleasure of her company for the past hour and more, after all."

Sir Frederick looked as if he would like to protest, but did not quite dare; the Duke of Ravenham was not a man lightly defied and he knew it well. The two men locked eyes for a moment, and then Sir Frederick nodded grudgingly.

"If you insist, Your Grace," he said at last, making a mockery of the title. "A lesser mortal like myself must stand aside, I see. Try not to forget me, Miss Gordon," he concluded, sketching a bow from the saddle.

"I will have the mare sent round within the hour, Sir Frederick," she said, uncertain how to react to this by-play. Why did these two gentlemen dislike each other so?

"As you wish," he said nonchalantly and set spur to his mount, leaving Brie alone with the duke.

"What were you doing out here alone with that fellow?" asked Ravenham abruptly before she could speak.

She blinked up at him in surprise. "Why, he called to take me riding. That is perfectly respectable, is it not? And we were not alone; the groom was there."

"*His* groom, I doubt not, who had conveniently disappeared. And while riding may be perfectly respectable, Sir Frederick More is not. It was shatterbrained, even for an innocent like yourself, to come out alone in his company like that. I would not have thought even Lady Platt would be blind to the risk."

"Risk? What risk?" Brie had convinced herself that she had imagined any menace in Sir Frederick's eyes a few moments ago. He certainly had behaved more pleasantly

than the duke! "Was he about to carry me off, do you
think? Sir Frederick behaved like a gentleman, which is
more than I can say for you, running him off like that!"

"You should be thanking me rather than attacking me,"
said the duke drily, a glimmer of amusement beginning to
appear in his rigid face. "It can do you no good whatever
to be seen in Sir Frederick's company, no matter how
smooth his manners appear to be. The man is a hardened
rake."

"He is a good friend of my sister's," said Brie primly.
"As it happens, he called to take both of us riding, but she
was unable to go." They were moving at a brisk trot
through the streets as they spoke, and were drawing near
to the Platt residence. "Come in and ask her if you do not
believe me, Your Grace," she finished with a challenging
glare.

"Oh, I believe you well enough. Your sister is not the
first married woman to have her name linked with Sir
Frederick's."

Brie looked at him in puzzlement for a moment, and
then colour flamed into her face as his meaning became
clear. "How dare you?" she demanded angrily.

"I apologise, Miss Gordon," he said quickly. "That
should not have been said to a young lady." What was the
matter with him? He had intended to warn the girl, to put
her on her guard, but certainly never to mention the possible relationship between Sir Frederick and Lady Platt.
Aside from the fact that such knowledge would be sure to
shock an innocent such as Miss Gordon obviously was, he
himself only knew of it through common gossip, and
therefore could place no dependence on its veracity.

Brie, meanwhile, had lapsed from righteous indignation on her sister's behalf into an embarrassed silence. The
embarrassment, however, was not so much at what His

Grace had implied as at the realisation that it might possibly be true, based on what she herself had seen and heard. At the very least, her sister had no doubt been indiscreet enough to give rise to speculation by the observant.

Hard on the heels of that thought, however, followed another: the memory of the Duke of Ravenham alone in the parlour of an inn in the company of a woman who was not his wife. How dared he censure her sister—or Sir Frederick—when he himself was just as bad? It was even possible that the woman had been some other man's wife though, remembering her appearance, she thought it far more likely that she had been one of those less-than-virtuous "ladies" that Sir Seymour had once referred to as "Cyprians." Not that it made any difference!

Her chin came up as she prepared to challenge him on that point, but as she opened her mouth, she realised that to do so would be to admit that previous meeting, which the duke seemed to have forgotten. He was regarding her expectantly, she belatedly realised.

"Do you wish to come in, Your Grace?" she finally asked rather lamely, glad that their arrival at the house provided an excuse for her to speak.

"No thank you, Miss Gordon. It has been my pleasure to be of service to you," he said meaningfully, making it obvious that he felt she should have thanked him for that service.

She looked daggers at him and his amusement deepened. "Good day, then, Your Grace," she said. Thank him? She felt more like throwing her crop at him!

By this time, one of the Platts' grooms had materialised to help her to dismount, and she did so in silence, wondering why the duke sat there watching her rather than taking himself off. Suddenly recollecting something, she turned to the groom.

"Please have this horse taken back to Sir Frederick More's stables. No doubt you can get his direction from someone."

"I knows it already, miss," said the young groom, with a half smile Brie was certain she did not like. She was afraid he might embellish his remark, so she forestalled him.

"Fine, then you should have no trouble," she said, pointedly dismissing the man. She was fuming at the fact that she had allowed the Duke of Ravenham to collect another piece of evidence against her sister. And still the infuriating duke did not leave!

"I find it curious," he drawled idly, a strange smile twisting his mouth, "that a girl who is so opposed to cruelty to animals could be at all attracted to a man like Sir Frederick, who is hardly known for his kindness to man or beast."

It took perhaps two seconds for the significance of his statement to strike Brie. "You knew? All this time you knew and never said a word?" Her anger was momentarily forgotten in sheer amazement.

"There could not be two girls in England with those remarkable turquoise eyes—united with the same outspokenness," he explained reasonably, obviously enjoying her chagrin. "Perhaps someday I'll invite you to my stables to observe for yourself how well I have heeded your strictures."

The knowledge that he was laughing at her served to rekindle her anger. "I hope you have, Your Grace," she retorted haughtily, her momentary embarrassment forgotten. "My views have not changed in the slightest, even if my gowns have."

"I'm glad to hear it," he replied, suddenly serious.
There was something in his eyes which caused her own to
fall, though this time not precisely with embarrassment.
He seemed to be silently probing her, she felt—but for
what?

"Try to take care, Miss Gordon," he said gently after a
slight pause during which she refused to meet his eyes. "I
would not have you hurt. The most vicious beasts in London are not animals, you know."

At this reference to the episode in the Park, her head
came back up defiantly. "Thank you for the warning," she
said sarcastically. "I will undertake to behave myself.
Again, I bid you good day, Your Grace."

With a smile, he touched his forehead to her in a mock
salute and rode away, leaving her on the doorstep. What an
infuriating man, she thought. His mood seemed to change
like lightning, so that she never knew where she stood with
him, or what he was thinking. There, just for a moment...

But no, she would allow no tenderness towards a man
who could so mistreat an animal—or even allow one of his
lackeys to do so, as she had begun to suspect had been the
case. Not that that excused him! Though, if he had indeed taken her strictures to heart, he might well be mend-
ing his ways.

Confused, but with her spirits unaccountably lighter,
Brie turned to walk up the front steps.

CHAPTER EIGHT

ALMACK'S WAS NOT quite what Brie had expected. True, the ladies and gentlemen present were as elegant as could be imagined, the men especially so in their formal knee-breeches. Everything and everyone seemed to exude pro-priety—though this perception might have been an effect of Angela's strict instructions on the behaviour expected in these sacrosanct rooms.

It was the rooms themselves which she found slightly disappointing, for they seemed quite ordinary. She had expected them to be papered and furnished with gold, at the very least, after the glowing encomiums she had re-ceived from her sister. During the ride here, the Duke of Ravenham had hinted that this would not be the case, but she had been too nervous about what amounted to her formal debut to pay him much heed.

Lady Platt had managed not to be in evidence when the duke called for her sister, perhaps doubting her ability to be civil under the crushing disappointment she felt at not being one of the party. Brie could not help but be grateful that she was thus spared any parting advice.

As they had entered the handsome, crested carriage, the duke had presented Brie to his sister, a pretty, unassuming girl with hair of a deeper brown than her own, who ap-peared to be near in age to herself. Brie had liked Lady Elizabeth at once and sensed that the feeling was mutual, but shyness, especially on Elizabeth's part, had thus far precluded much conversation.

Now, standing at the edge of the brightly lit ballroom of Almack's, Brie mentally compared her own gown to Lady Elizabeth's. Both were of a modest cut, suitable to their unmarried status, and boasted exquisite and expensive tailoring. While Brie's gown was of turquoise, midway between pale and vivid, Elizabeth's gown was pristine white, which suited her dark colouring admirably. Looking round the room, Brie noticed that white was by far the most popular colour for girls their age and could not regret that her gown stood a bit apart, while still being well within tasteful limits.

Before she could finish her detailed survey of the room and its inhabitants, a waltz was struck up and the Duke of Ravenham bowed over her hand.

"May I have the honour, Miss Gordon?"

"Is . . . is it all right?" Brie asked uncertainly. "My sister said . . ."

"I have obtained permission for you to waltz, if that is what you mean." He was regarding her with cool amusement, but she refused to let him anger her.

"In that case, Your Grace, I would be happy to dance with you." She was eager to join the couples on the floor for, of all the dances she had been learning over the past two weeks, the waltz was her favourite. It seemed so graceful, so much like floating, and besides, the music was beautiful.

The duke swung her onto the floor, belatedly hoping that she had been schooled in the steps, and was both surprised and delighted to discover that she waltzed as well as any lady he had ever danced with. Surely she could not have reached this degree of proficiency in the brief time she had been in London?

Dancing had, in fact, come quite easily to Brie, who was naturally graceful and had always led an active life. Her time spent helping with her father's practice had given her a gentle touch and a sense of timing often vital in judging one's reactions around unpredictable animals, both of which were of assistance on a dance floor, odd as it seemed. She was also not afraid, as so many debutantes might have been, of embarrassing herself by a misstep.

Just now she was discovering, however, that being held and twirled in the duke's arms was vastly different from dancing with the elderly and somewhat effeminate dancing master her sister had employed. She had never really noticed before the degree of physical closeness this dance demanded—a closeness which caused her heart to beat in a way not entirely accounted for by the exertions of the waltz. To divert her thoughts, she took refuge in conversation.

"I was pleased to make the acquaintance of the Lady Elizabeth, Your Grace," she began. Her voice sounded somewhat breathless, even to herself, but she thought she could reasonably hope he might think her winded by the dance. "She seems a charming girl."

"Yes, Elizabeth is the best of sisters. It would please me if you two were to become friends," he replied, which desire Brie could not help but find gratifying. He must not hold a grudge against her for the incident at the Ruby Crown—or the one in the Park—if he wanted her to associate with his sister, she thought, though she refused to analyse why his opinion of her should matter in the least.

"By the bye, that is what we are telling people, if they are curious about your arrival with us. That you are a friend of Elizabeth's," he explained to her questioning look. "After all, it would hardly do for it to be generally known that I am escorting you to pay off a wager." His tone was light, but Brie was stung by his words, nonetheless. She had almost managed to forget the reason for her presence here tonight, and that sudden reminder caused her to stiffen slightly in his arms.

"Indeed, Your Grace can consider it paid after tonight." Her voice had stiffened, as well.

"No, no," he returned, his tone still cheerful. "I agreed to see the job through, and I'm a man of my word."

They danced on in silence, Brie fighting an irrational disappointment at his words. Surely she had not expected him to say he was enjoying his obligation? Still, he might have said something of the sort out of common politeness, she thought, forgetting for the moment that she hated that sort of hypocrisy. Averting her face from the duke lest he somehow divine her thoughts, she looked across the room to see Sir Frederick More watching her from near the door.

She was conscious of a mixture of alarm and triumph at the sight of him. Alarm, because this was the first she had seen of him since that awkward moment in the Park, though she knew he had called on her sister at least once. Triumph, because his presence here must surely prove that his reputation could not be as bad as the duke had painted it.

As the dance ended, she saw that Sir Frederick, attired in sober black, was cautiously making his way towards her, and glanced quickly at the duke to see if he had noticed. His frown indicated that he had, though he said nothing.

Ravenham was as surprised as Brie had been to see Sir Frederick at Almack's, but not for the same reasons. He knew, as she did not, that the standards of conduct for gentlemen were much more lenient than those for ladies and that while the patronesses might deny a lady the entrée here on the basis of a mere hint of indiscretion, a gentleman had to be all but convicted of a crime to be cut in the same way. No, he was merely surprised that the notorious Sir Frederick would choose to spend an evening enjoying the tame pursuits offered at Almack's rather than at one of the more exotic establishments he generally haunted. What was the man playing at?

His thoughts were diverted by the press of people, mostly male, that met them as they left the dance floor, desirous of an introduction to the new Beauty. Looking at Miss Gordon thoughtfully, he had to admit with some surprise that she *was* beautiful. The turquoise gown matched her eyes precisely, emphasising their loveliness. And how could he ever have thought the rest of her face plain? It showed intelligence and animation, traits sadly lacking in most of the young ladies one met in London—and particularly at Almack's.

Brie was somewhat confused by the sudden attention, but the duke handled everything smoothly, introducing her to what seemed like several dozen people in the space of a few minutes. She was sure it would take her weeks to sort through the names, not to mention the titles. Was that Sir Clarence, now, or Lord Clarence? And the one who had said his name was Gardiner—was that Mr. or Lord Gardiner, or could that be the man's Christian name?

Angela had been right, she realised. Simply to be seen with the Duke of Ravenham was enough to bring her into fashion. Graciously promising dances to one young (or not so young) gentleman after another, she felt a touch on her arm and looked round.

"Save me one more, if it's not too late already," said the duke, his expression bland. "Preferably a waltz." She nodded and he walked away with a cool smile, leaving her to deal with her new admirers.

Dancing set after set, Brie was pleased to see that Lady Elizabeth appeared to be as popular as herself, never sitting down. They exchanged glances once or twice as they passed each other on the floor, and their budding friendship was silently strengthened. Watching the other girl, Brie tried idly to determine whether she seemed to be favouring one gentleman over the others, but could detect no sign of partiality in Elizabeth's manner.

Returning breathless from a country dance, Brie found herself next to an equally breathless Lady Elizabeth and suggested that they sit one out together, which proposal Elizabeth accepted with alacrity. Moving off to one side in search of a glass of the rather warm lemonade which was offered, they were halted by the Duke of Ravenham and another gentleman of about the same age.

"Miss Gordon, I'd like to present you to Lord Garvey, one of my closest friends. Barry, you already know my sister, Elizabeth."

Brie regarded the young man speculatively, realising that this must be the same Lord Garvey that the duke had lost the wager to, resulting in this opportunity for herself. Lord Garvey glanced keenly at her, but then turned to regard Lady Elizabeth with more than passing interest.

"This can't be the same little Lady Eliza that I remember, with the perpetual pigtails and muddy petticoat!" he exclaimed. There was admiration mixed with disbelief in both his tone and expression.

Glancing quickly at her new friend, Brie was startled to see a deep blush suffuse Elizabeth's delicate complexion. She retained enough composure to greet Lord Garvey with a shy smile, however, as well as a murmured response that he had changed, as well. The duke was frowning slightly, and to divert his attention, Brie broke the small silence which had descended.

"Lady Elizabeth and I were just going in search of some lemonade, Your Grace. Perhaps you and Lord Garvey would be kind enough to procure some for us."

She trembled a bit at her own outspokenness, but the two gentlemen seemed to find nothing out of the ordinary in the request and complied readily. The two girls found seats near the wall and awaited their return.

"I collect that you knew Lord Garvey when you were much younger," Brie said tentatively after a moment, in hopes of beginning a real conversation with the shy Elizabeth.

"Oh, yes," agreed her companion, almost eagerly. "He and Dexter were forever together, as our estates adjoined and they are of an age. Of course, I was just a silly little girl in their eyes, though I tried my best to keep up with them. I'm afraid I was a bit of a hoyden back then."

Brie felt herself warming more to this girl every moment and mentioned that she was country bred herself and only now learning how to go on in Society.

"I would never have guessed it!" exclaimed Elizabeth admiringly. "Why, it took four years at Miss Gebhart's Seminary and another abroad to give me what my brother and aunt decided was enough Town polish to make my come-out. I just hope I can remember it all."

"You terrify me!" returned Brie, her alarm not entirely assumed. "There must be gaping holes in my education, in that case. Right now, I'm only hoping to remember a few of the names I've learned tonight!"

Their conversation continued in that vein, and by the time the gentlemen returned, they were Eliza and Brie to each other and felt that they had known each other for years.

"Why is it you never mentioned what a Beauty your sister has grown up to be, Dex?" was Lord Garvey's first comment as soon as they were out of earshot.

"I guess I never noticed. You know how it is, one's own sister and all," he replied with a sidelong glance at his friend. "Never thought you were much in the petticoat line, anyway, Barry."

"Oh, I'm not," declaimed Garvey quickly. "Just couldn't help noticing the change in her, that's all. So," he continued, turning to other matters, "that's the Miss Gordon whose fate will determine your honour."

"My honour?" exclaimed Ravenham. "What the devil do you mean by that?"

"No need to fly into the boughs, old boy," Garvey said with a laugh. "I only meant that the payment of your wager—debt of honour, you know—hinges on her success."

"Do you foresee that I'll have any problem there?" he asked, his attention successfully diverted.

"Not if she goes on as she has begun. Seems a much more genteel girl than her sister, and dashed pretty, too." He had noticed her tact a moment ago in smoothing over an awkward situation, if Dexter had not. "Your sister seems to have taken to her," he added, glancing back to where the two girls sat, deep in conversation.

"Yes," agreed the duke, following Garvey's gaze with a slight frown.

"I thought it was what you wanted?" asked his friend, surprised at his expression. "By the bye, what story are you putting about? An old school chum of your sister's?"

"No, just an old friend. We wouldn't want some other chit from Miss Gebhart's establishment declaring to the world that she's never seen Miss Gordon before. Too risky."

Garvey looked at his companion with admiration. "I would never have thought of that," he admitted. "Good thing I asked before I started spreading the story."

"You always were a nodcock, Barry," replied Ravenham good-naturedly. "We'd best hurry if we're to get this stuff to the girls before the next set forms."

BY THE TIME they were ready to leave Almack's, after midnight, Brie no longer felt alone in London. She had made numerous acquaintances, even if she only counted those whose names she could match to faces, several admirers and one close friend in Lady Elizabeth. The only sour note had been provided by Sir Frederick but, she had to admit, it was not really his fault. It was the obvious friction between him and the duke which caused her discomfort.

The evening was nearly three-fourths gone before Sir Frederick approached her for a dance, and she had to regretfully inform him that she was already engaged for every one. She was truly disappointed, for she felt that dancing with Sir Frederick would show the duke that she was not to be bullied, but she was conscious of a vague sense of relief, as well, which she couldn't understand.

As the evening drew to a close, Brie (and Elizabeth) were besieged by gentlemen begging the honour of calling upon them the next day. Both girls looked to the Duke of Ravenham before answering these requests, and he benignly gave his assent to each one. Most were quite eligible in the light of suitors, and all were eminently respectable, so it must have been some devil which prompted his comment to Miss Gordon in a sarcastic undertone.

"No doubt you will manage to nab one or another of these fine fellows who are too besotted to enquire about your fortune. I wish you luck!"

Startled and hurt by his tone, for she had assumed he would be pleased by her success, Brie groped for a suitable rejoinder. Before she could form one, however, she found herself face to face with Sir Frederick More.

"Might I also have the honour of calling upon you, Miss Gordon? Perhaps you would do me the favour of walking out with me tomorrow." His air of assurance showed that he was aware that the duke could not very well deny him without giving rise to unwelcome speculation. Brie realised it, as well.

"Certainly, Sir Frederick," she answered without a glance at the duke. "I look forward to seeing you again." She was more pleased to have been so promptly revenged on the duke for his rudeness than at the prospect of entertaining Sir Frederick, but let no trace of that show in her voice.

Sir Frederick bowed and made his escape before His Grace could repent of his forbearance. Damn the man's insolence, thought the duke in frustration. And Miss Gordon was no better, deliberately flouting him like that. He maintained a disapproving silence as he escorted her and his sister to the waiting carriage, but as the two girls were gaily comparing notes on the evening it was doubtful whether either of them even noticed.

"I'M NOT CERTAIN I wish you to pursue Miss Gordon's acquaintance after all," Ravenham informed his sister abruptly as they departed that young lady's doorstep. He had continued his silence during the brief drive, but it had only served to demonstrate to him how rapidly the friendship between the two girls was flourishing. He found being ignored by a young lady a novel experience, and one he did not care for.

"Why, Dexter!" exclaimed Elizabeth in surprise. "I thought you wished us to be friends! And I must admit, I find her excessively agreeable. Whatever has caused you to change your mind?"

"We know scarcely anything about her," he responded loftily, aware that he really had no good argument to put forth. "Her sister often behaves in an ill-bred manner, and I would not wish you exposed to that."

"Oh, gammon!" returned Elizabeth, whose shyness did not extend to her own family. "We've been through all that and you know it! From what you have told me, you very likely know more about her family than she does herself, and Brie is certainly not ill bred, whatever her sister may be."

"Brie?" asked the duke, momentarily diverted.

"Miss Gordon. Brie is her family nickname, short for Gabriella, and she asked me to call her that when I told her to drop the 'Lady' from my name. Her father was Gabriel, you see, and by the time Brie was born her parents had despaired of a son, so she was named after him. Then her brother came along a few years later so, to avoid confusion, she became Brie and he is called Gabe."

"You seem to have gleaned quite a bit of family history yourself," remarked her brother sourly.

"Why, Dex! I do believe you're jealous! You're out of sorts because Brie—Miss Gordon—was so sought after this evening."

"Nonsense!" he replied, startled at the thought. Could that be it? Could he possibly be forming a *tendre* for the girl? "I don't wish to discuss it further," he said brusquely as Elizabeth appeared ready to continue the subject. "You may associate with her if you wish, but I pray you will not

introduce any of her vulgar relations into our household.''

Elizabeth agreed to abide by this compromise, as she
had no particular wish to become acquainted with the
Platts, but exacerbated her brother's ill humour by
chuckling quietly at intervals the rest of the way home, so
delighted was she with her discovery.

CHAPTER NINE

BRIE AWOKE near noon the next day, in tolerably good spirits but still tired from the night before. She wondered what was wrong with her; dancing for five hours might be strenuous, but surely no more strenuous than assisting at a difficult calving. Of course, she admitted, she had been tired the day after that, as well.

Entering the parlour in search of anyone else who might be awake, she was amazed to see a veritable garden containing every imaginable colour and variety of flower which, on closer inspection, proved to be more than a dozen bouquets, all addressed to herself! No wonder Angela was not in evidence, she thought wryly, inspecting the various cards, then chided herself for such an uncharitable thought.

After reading every card, she was conscious of a faint sense of disappointment that none was from the Duke of Ravenham. Why, even Lord Garvey had sent a bouquet, and she had no illusions about where that young man's affections lay! This thought led naturally to Elizabeth, and she felt a sudden eagerness to see her new friend again. Had she received so many flowers? Brie hoped so.

Suddenly conscious that she had had no breakfast, although it was nearer time for luncheon, Brie repaired to the dining room, where eggs, ham, toast and coffee had been left on the sideboard. She had just seated herself, a well-heaped plate before her, when Angela entered, superbly dressed and coiffed as usual and not looking at all as though she had just risen.

"Not much worried about your figure, are you?" she asked caustically, with a gesture towards Brie's repast. "Though, if anything, you could use some plumping out, I suppose."

Brie refused to have her day ruined by her sister's acid tongue and mildly bade her good-morning. She diplomatically refrained from asking whether she had yet been in the parlour—she rather suspected, from her sour mood, that she had. A breakfast not much less generous than her own seemed to go a long way towards improving Lady Platt's outlook, however, and as she was finishing she finally enquired about Brie's evening at Almack's.

"As you stayed fairly late, I suppose it is safe to assume that your debut was something of a success?" The question was asked casually, but Brie could sense her sister's anxiety over the answer.

"Yes, I believe so," she answered cautiously, not sure just what Angela wished to hear. "I met a great number of people and danced most of the evening."

Lady Platt relaxed slightly, and Brie realised that her sister must actually have been worried that something would go wrong. *Perhaps she really does care a bit about me,* she was thinking, when Angela's next words dispelled that illusion.

"Thank God you did nothing to embarrass us, then! You must have followed my advice and kept your mouth shut. The gentlemen seem to appreciate that in a lady, I've noticed."

"No, I did *not* keep my mouth shut," replied Brie, bristling at her sister's tone, "and the gentlemen seemed to appreciate me, anyway. You have not yet seen the parlour, I take it?"

"Oh, I have no doubt the gentlemen, and the ladies, too, were eager to ingratiate themselves with you, as you came in on Ravenham's arm. There are few who would not benefit by his notice." Lady Platt showed a fine disregard for her own behaviour, little short of grovelling, towards the duke. "I only hope that you said nothing that might reflect poorly on *me*. Don't forget to whom you owe this visit, missie."

"I don't recall that I mentioned you at all, Angela," replied Brie drily, "so you need not worry. Word is bound to get about that I am your sister, but you can depend upon me not to spread it."

This was not what Lady Platt had meant at all, as she had every hope of being associated with Gabriella's success, and she sought to undo the harm her jealousy had wrought.

"Now, now, my dear," she soothed. "I didn't for a moment mean that I am *ashamed* of you, only that I was concerned that you might embarrass yourself, being so new to Town and its ways. I am sorry if I was a bit sharp, but I fear I have the headache most dreadfully and it has put me a bit out of temper. Now come, let us remove to the parlour, for if I am not much mistaken you will have simply droves of callers today!"

Brie had a shrewd suspicion as to the reason for this sudden *volte-face*, but obediently followed her sister out of the room.

LADY PLATT had been quite correct, for within fifteen minutes the parlour was besieged by several of the gentlemen that Brie had met the evening before. Her sister played the perfect Society hostess, the effect only slightly marred when she succumbed to the temptation to flirt, and Brie found that she had less trouble than she had expected remembering names.

There was Lord Hugely, a slight man whose appearance was enough at odds with his name to make it easy to remember, and Mr. Beakerton, whose long, pointed nose similarly jogged her memory. Sir Jeffrey she remembered by his stutter, and Lord Billings by the brightness of his waistcoat, though it was a vivid pink today rather than the brilliant orange it had been last night.

And then there was Lord Timothy Gardiner, who had been her most persistent admirer at Almack's, so much so that she had with difficulty persuaded him against the advisability of a third dance. He was very handsome, with his black curling locks and aquiline features, though small of stature and probably no older than herself.

"I see you received my offering, Goddess, and have kept it within your sight!" he exclaimed upon entering, gesturing towards the largest of the floral arrangements.

Brie reflected that she had had little choice in the matter, as there was surely no cupboard in the house large enough to contain it, but thanked him sweetly just the same. She had noticed how Angela's eyes had widened when his name was announced, and concluded that he must be a person of more consequence than she had realised.

"Pray allow me to place myself at your feet," he continued, but Brie stopped him before he could actually sit upon the floor.

"Please, my lord, no," she said gently but firmly. "There is a perfectly adequate chair right here, and I would much prefer you to sit there."

"Anything to please the divine Miss Gordon," he acquiesced, moving to the chair indicated. He then lapsed into silence, his whole attention riveted on her face, oblivious even to Lady Platt's most determined efforts to draw him into her conversation with Mr. Beakerton.

Brie suspected that he might be composing more of the rather astonishing poetry he had shared with her last night at Almack's, and hoped that his quarter of an hour might end before he completed it. That wish was apparently answered, for when he rose to leave, his knitted brows indicated that he was still deep in thought; he broke his trance only long enough to kiss her fingertips lingeringly and utter a heartfelt sigh at the parting.

After a hectic hour, Brie and Angela finally found themselves alone in the parlour, able to catch their breath. Brie had to admire the way her sister had been able to keep every one of their callers entertained, never favouring one too obviously over another, and never losing her composure, even in the face of near-pandemonium when the tea tray had been accidentally overturned by Mr. Simkins. Brie herself had been hard-pressed not to laugh when cream and strawberry had sadly marred both his satin hose and his dignity.

"Well!" Angela exclaimed as the door closed behind the last caller. "You have taken, and no mistake! I'll be very surprised if even *you* can't contrive to bring one of those bucks up to scratch!" Her smile was genuine, Brie realised. "I advise you to do it quickly, before your lack of fortune becomes generally known."

This reminded Brie all too forcibly of the duke's words to her last night. "I have no intention of wedding anyone at this point," she informed her sister tartly, "and if I did, I certainly wouldn't do it so dishonestly as that! I have never so much as implied that I have a fortune."

"Of course not, my dear, how should you?" asked Angela, startled that her sister should have taken offence at what she had intended as a compliment. "But anyone seeing you in public with Ravenham is bound to assume it. By the bye, what tale was given out to account for your presence with him last night?"

"That I was an old friend of his sister's," replied Brie grudgingly. The thought that she might rightly be accused of such deceit disturbed her profoundly.

"There you have it, then! No pauper is likely to be a lifelong friend of the Lady Elizabeth! By all accounts, she is too proud to even speak to anyone with less than twenty thousand a year."

"What a nasty thing to say!" exclaimed Brie, springing instantly to the defence of her friend. "Elizabeth is by far the pleasantest person I have yet met in London, and she knows full well I'm not wealthy! The only flaw she might possibly have is in being a bit shy."

"My apologies, my dear," said Angela quickly, startled again. "I've never met the girl myself, and was only repeating what I had heard. It is still true, however, that her appearing to be your friend will only go to reinforce the idea of your eligibility, and we should do all we can to take advantage of it."

Brie was about to insist that Elizabeth truly *was* her friend, choosing to ignore the latter half of Angela's statement, when Sir Frederick More was announced. Lady Platt pinned on her most charming smile in greeting, though it became somewhat fixed when Sir Frederick gave her only a perfunctory greeting before turning to her sister.

"You haven't forgotten your promise to walk out with me, I hope, Miss Gordon?" His manner was solicitous without being too familiar, and his appearance was every inch the gentleman in pearl grey jacket, buckskins and blindingly polished Hessians.

Brie, suddenly realising that she had neglected to mention to Angela his presence last night at Almack's, glanced
nervously at her sister. "I...I haven't yet...that is, would
it be all right, Angela?"

Lady Platt's eyes had narrowed dangerously, but her
voice was silkily pleasant. "Of course, my dear, but pray
take your abigail for appearance' sake." She watched silently as Brie left the room to comply with this suggestion, then turned to Sir Frederick.

"And when was this assignation made, may I ask?" she
enquired waspishly, her fine blue eyes fairly shooting
sparks.

"Why, last night at Almack's, my dear," he replied
tranquilly, "and it is hardly an assignation, as it was made
in front of at least a dozen people, to include our dashing
duke."

"You don't care for him, I have noticed," she commented. "Are you jealous, perchance?"

"Only of his wealth, my dear, unless you are inclined to
favour him."

"Would it vex you if I did?" she asked coquettishly,
leaning slightly forward so that her charms were more
prominently displayed.

"Indubitably." He was moving to seat himself on the
settle next to her when Brie returned, abigail in tow.

"We'll discuss it on my return," he promised with a half
wink and lightly touched her fingertips with his lips. "Shall
we go, Miss Gordon?"

The streets of Mayfair were fairly crowded, as the
weather was fine, and they proceeded at a leisurely pace.
Brie had been vaguely nervous at the prospect of being
nearly alone with Sir Frederick for the first time since their
ride in the Park, but he maintained a polite flow of small
talk which soon had her laughing at her fears as well as his

banter. The Duke of Ravenham had surely been misinformed! Besides, she thought with a smile, what could the man possibly do in front of so many witnesses?

"So you enjoyed that story, did you?" asked Sir Frederick, having noticed the smile.

"Oh, vastly," replied Brie, somewhat confusedly, as she had not been paying full attention. She wondered what it had been about, as he was regarding her rather strangely. To change the subject, she exclaimed over a horse just then passing.

"What fine lines that gelding has, don't you agree, Sir Frederick?"

"You are indeed a good judge of horseflesh, Miss Gordon," he agreed. "Until a fortnight since, that horse belonged to the Prince himself. Which reminds me—" he regarded her intently "—I have arranged to have the filly you rode last week stabled at the Platts' so that you can have free use of her."

Brie flushed with mingled embarrassment and indignation. "I would much rather you did not," she said flatly.

"Nonsense, my dear, easier for you, easier for me. No trouble at all, I assure you." There was a gleam in his eye now which she could not mistake.

"Pray do not make it impossible for me to appreciate your kindness to me thus far, Sir Frederick. I shall have her returned to you at once if I find her there." Both tone and expression convinced her companion that she was in earnest.

They walked on in silence for some moments, Sir Frederick wearing a frustrated scowl. Brie did not notice, as she was taking care not to look in his direction until her temper cooled, unwilling to quarrel with such a good friend of her sister's. She resented the fact that he seemed to credit her with so little sense, but fought the temptation to tell him so.

Her averted gaze sharpened as it took in a half-grown black kitten coming towards them along the railings. The poor thing looked badly malnourished, and she wished she dared take it home to feed it. Since coming to London she had seen many flagrant cases of animal abuse which she had been unable to do anything about, and it made her all the more desirous of helping this furry little urchin.

The kitten stopped to sniff hopefully at a doorstep, but apparently found no odours of interest, for it continued on its way. Just as it drew level with them, Brie made the quiet clucking noise which she had often used to call the barn cats to her, and the tiny creature perked up its ears and came timidly towards the sound.

Sir Frederick, in a less than amiable frame of mind, just then noticed the animal for the first time. Muttering an oath, he vented his feelings by kicking out at it with one of his gleaming Hessians. The kitten sailed through the air and hit the iron railings with a thud.

With a cry of outrage and dismay, Brie hurried to crouch next to the injured cat. It tried to rise shakily, but it was obvious that one of its back legs had been hurt and it mewed piteously. She folded it carefully into the embroidered shawl she was carrying and lifted it gently, crooning to it all the while. Sir Frederick watched the process in surprise and some amusement.

"What, pray, do you intend to do with that, Miss Gordon?" he enquired lazily as she stood up. "Better to leave the thing in the gutter where it belongs. I daresay it won't live long, anyway."

She turned towards him and the loathing in her eyes made him flinch. She was fairly quivering with rage. "How dare you even say such a thing when it is you who have practically killed it?" she demanded. "Get away from me, you brute!" she exclaimed, when he put out a hand towards her burden. "Don't you dare touch this poor kitten again!"

"Miss Gordon, you are overwrought," he began, in a feeble attempt to retrieve the situation, but she cut him off.

"Overwrought! You…you are despicable! You had best leave me, sir, before I become 'overwrought' enough to do you an injury! I will contrive to get home without your escort; indeed, I should feel infinitely safer without it!" She turned on her heel and walked quickly back the way they had come, the bewildered abigail fairly trotting to keep up.

Sir Frederick glowered at her retreating back, cursing this unexpected snag in his plans. How was he to know the girl had some ridiculous sentimentality about cats? And how dared the little nobody speak to him thus? Somehow, he would have to bring the saucy little wench to her senses—at least in regards to himself!

CHAPTER TEN

BRIE REACHED her sister's house a few minutes later to discover that the Lady Elizabeth had but that moment arrived and was in the parlour with Lady Platt. She shrugged in resignation—gently, to avoid disturbing the now sleeping kitten—and entered the room Madsen had indicated. If she and Elizabeth were going to be friends, she would surely learn sometime about her tenderness for animals. As for her sister, well, she had never really had *her* good opinion!

"Why, here you are already!" exclaimed Lady Platt as Gabriella came through the door. "I was just telling Lady Elizabeth that you might be gone for—" She stopped in mid-sentence, suddenly catching sight of her sister's burden. "Whatever is that? A *cat?* And what have you done to your shawl?"

Brie carefully seated herself near Elizabeth before answering. "Yes, it is a cat, a kitten, actually, and injured. I could hardly have left it on the street, so I brought it with me."

Angela's face turned bright pink with the effort of restraining herself from saying all that propriety forbade in front of their guest. Elizabeth, meanwhile, was regarding the sleeping kitten with sympathetic interest.

"Poor little thing!" she said. "How badly is it injured, Brie, do you know?"

"Not yet." Brie warmed to her new friend all the more at this show of concern. "I had planned to take it up to my bedchamber and examine it there. Would you care to come with me?"

"Certainly!" agreed Elizabeth, rising. "That is, if you have no objection, ma'am?" she asked, turning towards her hostess.

"No, no, you girls go on," said Lady Platt tightly, clinging to her smile with iron control. *Just wait until I get that hoyden alone,* she was thinking fiercely.

The two younger ladies went upstairs, leaving Angela in the parlour to agonise over the impression the Lady Elizabeth must be receiving and to wonder what could have happened to Sir Frederick. She would have a thing or two to say to *that* gentleman when next she saw him, as well!

"What a lovely room!" was Elizabeth's first comment upon entering Brie's bedchamber. "Where do you want to set the kitten—on the bed?" she then asked practically.

"No, I think the dressing table might be better," Brie replied. "Then I can be seated while I look at his leg." Setting the kitten down gently with one arm, she swept aside the clutter of small bottles and brushes which normally lived on the table. The kitten awakened during this process and gazed round at its new surroundings. Apparently satisfied, it licked its shoulder with a tiny pink tongue and began to purr.

"He doesn't seem to be in much pain now, at least," ventured Elizabeth.

"No, he doesn't," agreed Brie, unwrapping the shawl. "I don't believe the leg is broken," she said after a brief examination, during which the kitten batted playfully at her probing fingers, "but it is certainly badly bruised, and cut a bit just here." She pointed at a spot above the paw where some blood had apparently oozed onto the black fur.

"Can I do anything to help?" asked Elizabeth. She was finding this situation far more interesting than the typical social call and had, besides, an innate sympathy for animals which she shared with her new friend—and her brother.

"Would you dip this in the ewer over there so I can wash the cut?" asked Brie, handing her a scrap of cotton cloth she had pulled from one of the dressing table drawers. From the same drawer, she lifted a jar of the salve she had used on the unfortunate horse at the Ruby Crown.

"My father was always very good with animals," explained Brie, mindful of Angela's concern over revealing his profession. "He taught me some of what he knew." When Elizabeth crossed back to her with the wet cloth she expertly cleansed the wound, applied the salve and wrapped it in another of the cotton cloths, talking soothingly to the kitten and cheerfully to Elizabeth during the process. At length she was done.

"There," she said to the kitten with satisfaction. "You should do quite well now, if I can persuade my sister to let you stay."

"Perhaps you should ask her in my presence," suggested Elizabeth wickedly, not having missed Lady Platt's obsequious manner towards herself.

"An excellent notion," replied Brie, laughing, and the two girls descended to complete their errand of mercy.

"NOT THAT YOU LEFT ME any choice," Lady Platt was saying indignantly. "I could hardly refuse in front of the Lady Elizabeth without seeming churlish!"

Elizabeth had departed, her ploy to force Angela to agree to the kitten's continued residence in the Platt household having been successful. Since then, Brie had been listening to her sister's tirade on her want of breeding and proper gratitude and was beginning to tire of it.

"I don't believe Elizabeth was the least bit offended to help me tend to the poor thing," she interposed calmly, when Angela paused to think up more offences which Brie might be guilty of. "In fact, I got the distinct impression that she was enjoying herself."

"Yes, we must be thankful for that, I suppose, but you could not have known that in advance." A sudden thought seemed to strike her. "Never tell me you told the Lady Elizabeth of our father's profession!"

"No, I only said that he had been good with animals, though it seemed disloyal as well as dishonest not to mention the extensive training and experience he'd had. There were probably no more than half a dozen veterinaries in all of England who could have come close to his skill."

"Be that as it may, I will repeat to you what I said before: if his profession were to become generally known, we would find ourselves cut by everyone who matters in Society. And that includes your fine new friends, as well! When I think how ill bred, how *common* you looked, coming in here off the street, quite alone, and carrying that thing, I feel ready to sink! By the bye, why *were* you alone? What happened to Sir Frederick? You must know it is not at all..."

"Angela, I will thank you not to mention that man's name again in my presence." Brie's calm had broken and her voice was suddenly deadly. "If you feel the need to blame this incident, which apparently came so close to ruining us, on anyone, you can blame him. That poor kitten was minding its own business, searching for scraps of food, no doubt, when that... that *monster* kicked it, for no reason whatever. As I no longer felt safe in his presence, and

certain that he would not be safe in mine, I came back here
to tend to the injury *he* caused.''

Her anger had returned in full force at the memory, and
Angela simply sat there, dumbfounded at her sister's vehemence. She knew from long experience that there was no
point in trying to reason with her—their father had been
just the same when he had perceived any so-called cruelty
towards an animal. She still winced at the recollection of
the time he had caught her tormenting a chained dog with
a stick when she was a child. Before she could gather her
wits enough to give her sister a proper set-down for her
insolence, Brie had left the room.

ELIZABETH, MEANWHILE, was reflecting on the scene just
past as she drove herself home. She felt drawn to Brie as
she had not been to another girl of her own age since leaving Miss Gebhart's Seminary and her old school fellows.
The other young ladies "out" in Society seemed
so...*shallow* in comparison to her. She sincerely hoped
that Dexter would come to his senses before some other
young buck snapped her up. Brie would make such a delightful sister!

On that thought, as if on cue, she looked up to see her
brother and Lord Garvey walking a little way ahead.
Slowing the curricle, she greeted them cheerfully, only the
slightest flush betraying her consciousness of the admiration in Garvey's eyes.

"May I offer you gentlemen a lift home, or had you
other plans on so fine a day?'' she asked after they had
exchanged pleasantries.

"No, we have concluded our business, such as it was,
and were on our way home to sustain ourselves before
venturing out again,'' replied the duke. "I'd as lief ride as
walk, myself; how about you, Barry?''

Lord Garvey acquiesced quickly, his eyes never leaving Elizabeth's piquant face, and the gentlemen climbed up to join her. Elizabeth gave the reins into the groom's hands so that she could chat comfortably with her companions and they resumed their short journey.

"And where have you been today, Eliza?" asked Dexter after a moment. "Not shopping, apparently, for I see no parcels."

"No, I have just been calling on Miss Gordon," replied Elizabeth, watching his face closely. It told her exactly nothing, for he kept it carefully blank.

After a brief debate with herself, she went on. "The most extraordinary thing happened while I was there." She proceeded to recount the episode with the injured kitten in full detail, to the amusement of the gentlemen. Knowing her brother's interest in and compassion for animals, she was hoping to increase his regard for her friend with the tale, but was uncertain whether she had succeeded.

"She applied a salve, you say," he interrupted her at one point. "How came she by it, do you know?"

"She said it had been a favourite of her father's, and that she always kept a jar of it by her for just such a need," answered Elizabeth, wondering why he should have fixed on such a minor matter.

He nodded, and she went on with her story, but he was thinking back to the incident at the inn and the horse's carefully treated wounds. He had thanked the groom at the Ruby Crown for his care and thought no more of it, but he had thought at the time that the man had looked confused at his thanks, as if he were not responsible. This might well explain that small mystery.

"And Lady Platt consented to the addition of a cat to her household?" asked Lord Garvey with a laugh when the tale was completed.

"I fear I gave her little choice," smiled Elizabeth. "I felt sure she would refuse if Brie, er, Miss Gordon waited until I had gone, so I suggested that she ask in my presence. And it worked! Lady Platt would not be thought heartless for the world, it would appear, which may go a long way towards explaining her sister's visit to London."

Ravenham had wondered about that himself, and was inclined to agree with his sister. Lady Platt was the worst toadeater he had encountered in some time, and he had encountered quite a few; it was obvious that the good opinion of the ton was of supreme importance to her. *Pity she can't see herself as she appears to others,* he thought. No doubt she'd be appalled.

"I take it I need not fear you will be striking up a friendship with Miss Gordon's sister, then," he teased Elizabeth.

She answered him with a grimace before speaking, this time taking a slightly different tack. "I have promised to take Miss Gordon driving soon, and perhaps to teach her to drive a pair, as she has never had opportunity to handle the ribbons before. But perhaps, Dex, as you are the better driver, she would learn more if you were to tutor her yourself?" Her expression was innocence itself.

He regarded her suspiciously for a moment, but then considered the suggestion seriously and discovered that he was not at all averse to such an enterprise. "Perhaps I should," he drawled finally. "But feel free to take her driving, by all means; I should think she'd be grateful for any excuse to escape that house."

A few days later, Brie was looking forward eagerly to her drive with the Lady Elizabeth, as she wished to apprise her of the kitten's progress, as promised, and to relate a few amusing stories of its antics to the one person who might appreciate them. It was wonderful to have found such a friend in London! She had begun to believe that Society ladies cared for nothing but the cut of their gowns and the latest gossip, but that was certainly not true of Elizabeth. She felt that in her new friend she had found a kindred spirit.

Glancing at the parlour clock, she realised that it was past the time Elizabeth had set and hoped that nothing had occurred to postpone their drive. At that moment, however, the bell sounded and a few seconds later Madsen entered the parlour to announce her guest.

"His Grace, the Duke of Ravenham," he droned in properly bored tones.

The duke entered even as Brie started to her feet in some dismay. "My apologies, Miss Gordon, for taking you by surprise like this," he said smoothly. "I fear Elizabeth was unable to come, so I offer myself as replacement. I hope I do not disappoint you unduly."

"No, ah, not at all, Your Grace," stammered Brie, caught completely off her guard. "I—I hope your sister is not taken ill?"

"Oh, no, Elizabeth is in perfect health," returned the Duke, suddenly seeming ill-at-ease. He hesitated a moment, then said, "To do her justice, she very much wished to come, but I persuaded her that I might make a better driving teacher than she. Elizabeth has only recently learned to handle the ribbons in public herself, you understand."

He wondered at himself for feeling any need to make excuses for his presence; why not come out and admit that he was here because he wanted to be, and for no other reason? But he did not do so.

"She will no doubt call upon you this afternoon or tomorrow, at any rate," he finished quickly. "She seemed desirous of speaking with you."

"I shall look forward to that," answered Brie sincerely.
Though disappointed to have her talk with Elizabeth
delayed, she could not suppress a surge of excitement at the
thought of the duke himself teaching her to drive, though
she tried. After all, she told herself, he doubtless intended
it only as one more payment towards clearing his "debt"
to Lord Garvey.

As if to bear out this explanation, once they were driving through the Park (with His Grace still in possession of
the reins) it became obvious that being seen with him so
publicly was certainly furthering the plan of bringing her
into fashion. No less than a dozen fashionably dressed
people, several of whom Brie recognised by this time,
stopped them to exchange greetings, seeming not at all
surprised to see them together.

"Such a charming couple you make!" exclaimed Lady
Billings, an elderly but extremely sharp-eyed matron with
a reputation for outspokenness. She had waved them down
with a peremptory flick of her handkerchief, having heard
about the newcomer from her son, and now leaned out of
her carriage window to observe them with obvious approval.

"You may suffer some backbiting from the disappointed hopefuls and their mamas, Miss Gordon, but you
mustn't mind that. I vow, it's a delight to see some of those
cats going green! Don't forget me when the invitations go
out!" With a parting flap of the handkerchief, she nodded to her groom and proceeded on her circuit of the Park.

Brie sat open-mouthed in dismay. Fearfully, she glanced
at the duke, certain that he would be furious, but saw with
relief that he merely looked amused.

"That old busybody revels in figuring out the latest *on
dits* before they happen," he remarked, chuckling. "The
fact that she's usually wrong doesn't seem to deter her in

the least. I hope she hasn't upset you with such talk, Miss Gordon," he continued, regarding her white face with some concern. "I assure you that most people pay very little attention to her maunderings."

"But some undoubtedly do," she said, finally finding her voice. "I hope I haven't put you in an awkward position, Your Grace." Despite his assurances, Brie still felt ready to die from embarrassment.

"Nothing I can't get out of," he said confidently. "Besides, *you* can hardly take the blame for any of this. That, I think, can be fairly apportioned between Garvey, myself and Sir Seymour. You might as well simply enjoy yourself."

Brie regarded him suspiciously but, realising that he apparently meant what he said—for the moment, anyway—she decided not to comment. She *had* been enjoying herself, actually, and would not let that interfering dowager spoil it, she told herself firmly.

The duke stopped the curricle shortly thereafter and silently offered Brie the reins. Nervously, she took them, more afraid of making a fool of herself in front of her companion than of losing control of the horses. There was a stretch of relatively empty path before them, which at least made it unlikely that anyone would be hurt if she proved inadequate to the task.

"Light, yet firm," he advised in the tone of a practised instructor, which indeed, he was, for many a young buck had prevailed upon him, through favour or wager, to share a small portion of his expertise with the ribbons. "It is really not so very different from guiding a horse which you are riding. The controls are essentially the same, only you must be continually aware of two beasts rather than just the one."

Proceeding, first at a walk and then at a sedate trot, Brie realised that he was right. He complimented her on her quickness as a pupil (quite sincerely, for he had taught thirty-year-old men who were far more hamhanded) and she fairly glowed.

She was looking particularly fetching today, Ravenham thought, in a pale blue jaconet carriage dress edged in deep turquoise. Even her hair seemed to have a most particular sheen. Before he could put such thoughts into words, however, a greeting was called out to them.

"Ah, Miss Gordon, Ravenham, good morning!"

Turning instinctively at her name, Brie encountered the cold, mocking glance of Sir Frederick More, whom she had not seen since the dreadful incident with the poor kitten. He was on foot, walking with three other fashionable people whom she did not know, two ladies and a gentleman.

The Duke of Ravenham returned the greeting with a noticeable lack of warmth but Brie, almost without thinking, flicked a glance at Sir Frederick, nodded politely to his companions and urged the horses into a trot. Sir Frederick stared after her in disbelief; the chit had given him the cut direct, and in public!

"I know I warned you against that fellow, but wasn't that a bit extreme?" asked the duke when they were well out of earshot.

Brie had not yet mentioned Sir Frederick's involvement in the episode with the kitten to anyone but her sister, but she temporarily forgot that.

"It was no more than he deserved, and a good deal less," she responded with a frown.

Angry colour suffused the duke's face, taking Brie by surprise, as did the sudden vehemence of his tone. "Has that blackguard insulted you in some way?" he demanded. "By God, I'll—" He broke off, choked with rage at what he was imagining.

Realisation struck Brie; the duke had no idea why she had cut the man, and appeared ready to call him out to defend her honour or some such thing! She saw that she would have to correct this misapprehension quickly, for he was already reaching for the reins with the apparent intention of going after Sir Frederick at once.

"Your Grace, please! No, he hasn't insulted me, not exactly. He has just shown himself for the brute he is, and I hope never to see him again."

She was about to relate the story of Sir Frederick's vicious attack on the kitten when her attention was drawn away by the sight of a stunning phaeton, apparently lacquered in pure gold, with an equally stunning occupant. Where had she seen that dark-haired beauty before? Sudden colour stained her cheeks as she recognised the duke's companion from the Ruby Crown!

Following her gaze, the duke immediately understood the reason for Miss Gordon's blush—but what could he say? Surveying Mademoiselle Monique with a critical eye he realised that despite her dazzling beauty, the Cyprian no longer held the slightest attraction for him. She had obviously found a protector of sufficient means to appeal to her, judging by that phaeton—one of the Royals, perhaps? But the thought bothered him not at all.

He turned back to Brie to find her watching him and self-consciously realised how his examination of Mademoiselle Monique might be interpreted, however wrongly.

"Miss Gordon, I—" he began, determined to somehow reassure the girl beside him, but she cut him off.

"Please, Your Grace," she said in a tight voice as she returned the reins to him, "I should like to go home. It grows late."

They drove back to the Platt residence in silence, the duke wondering what Brie had been going to say about Sir Frederick and she wondering what sort of explanation he could have been going to offer about his mistress. Both shot occasional furtive glances at the other during the drive, each trying to think of a casual way to reopen one or both topics, but no word was spoken.

Brie kept remembering the long look he had given the beautiful woman in the golden phaeton, and the more she thought about it the more certain she became that it was a lover's look. She reminded herself that she had no shadow of a right to question him about it, but that thought only depressed her further.

The duke, meanwhile, was trying to think of anything Sir Frederick might have done which would merit the comprehensive snub Brie had given him, but that she was unwilling to call an ''insult.'' Could whatever it was have been partly her own fault? She was so innocent—might she have precipitated a flirtation more serious than she had intended, he wondered.

They parted with cool formality, the Duke of Ravenham promising another lesson in the near future. Brie tried to draw what comfort she could from his words, but as she slowly mounted the broad front steps of the Platt town house she couldn't help feeling that the drive, which had begun so well, had turned out an unmitigated disaster.

CHAPTER ELEVEN

LADY PLATT'S HOPES, meanwhile, seemed in a fair way to being realised. There could be no doubt that her young sister's popularity was spilling over onto herself with gratifying results. While Almack's was still closed to her, she had begun to receive a few flattering invitations to events which she would have been excluded from last Season; Lady Bellerby's ball tonight, for instance! Everyone who was anyone was sure to be there, and she was to be a part of it. She was almost—but not quite—moved to thank Gabriella for such a turn of events. She nodded at her reflection in satisfaction, admiring the effect of her golden curls against the rose silk of her gown, and went to find her husband, who was to escort them this evening.

Sir Seymour's door opened at her tap, and there he stood, looking better than he had in years, though she would still not be so rash as to call him handsome. He also seemed unexpectedly sober.

"Almost ready, my dear?" he drawled pleasantly. He, too, was enjoying their sudden elevation in Society.

"Quite," she replied, still slightly surprised at his almost elegant appearance. True, his waistcoat and cravat still bespoke the dandy, but he was not dishevelled in the least and his coat was of a fairly sober royal blue.

"I'll ring for the carriage, then. Do you make certain Gabriella is ready."

They were to meet the Duke of Ravenham at the Bellerby ball, as the Platts had received an invitation and it would have looked odd if Miss Gordon did not accompany them. No doubt the duke would still pay a flattering amount of attention to her, however, as the wager terms were still in effect. Lady Platt rather hoped that attention would extend to a dance with Miss Gordon's sister.

For her own part, Brie was torn between anticipation and dread of the evening ahead. Anticipation, because she was actually beginning to enjoy her busy social schedule, especially when it included Elizabeth, as tonight's event would. She steadfastly refused to think about Elizabeth's brother, whom she had not seen since their awkward drive in the Park two days ago. The dread she admitted to herself stemmed from the fact that this would be the first such occasion where she would be accompanied by the Platts. She devoutly hoped that her sister might refrain from embarrassing her, though she did not go so far as to depend on it.

She had acceded to Angela's suggestion by wearing her rose silk, and felt she looked well enough. Her hair was fresh from Monsieur Philippe's hands and cascaded down her back in a riot of golden brown curls, stopping just short of her tiny waist. Opening the door to the hallway, she nearly walked into her sister, who was coming to fetch her.

Angela, she noted, was wearing a gown of nearly the same hue as her own, though of a far less modest cut. So that was why she had suggested the rose! Brie fumed, though she said nothing. No one could fail to notice Lady Platt's more voluptuous charms and pale blonde beauty and to draw the inevitable comparison between the sisters. Brie suddenly wished there was time to change her gown, but of course there was not. She had been unfavourably compared with Angela all her life (except by her father, of course) but the inevitable still had the power to sting.

"My dear! How charming you look!" gushed Lady Platt at the sight of her sister. And it was true, she realised in some dismay. Perhaps this idea of almost-matching gowns had not been such a good one, after all!

"Seymour is below with the carriage. Let us hurry," she said, with only the slightest of frowns.

Brie had to admit that Angela's attitude towards herself had certainly improved since invitations had begun to include her. She supposed that this more pleasant atmosphere in the household was worth a bit of embarrassment.

AFTER HER DISAPPOINTMENT at the appearance of Almack's, Brie had been careful not to set her expectations for Lady Bellerby's ballroom too high. Thus, she was positively dazzled at the room which greeted them once they were announced. The ballroom was of magnificent proportions, and so brightly lit that it seemed every candle in London must have been purchased for the occasion.

As they were among the last to arrive, the ball was already a decided "crush," although the dancing had not yet begun. Brie wondered how she would ever find Elizabeth—or the duke—in the jostling throng. The colourful array of dresses, turbans and feathers bewildered her eyes so that it was difficult to focus on the individuals who made up the crowd.

She need not have worried. Only moments after the announcement of, "Sir Seymour, Lady Platt and Miss Gordon," she saw the duke's imposing figure as he made his way towards her. He was easy to spot, after all, being a good half a head taller than nearly every other gentleman in the room.

"Miss Gordon!" he exclaimed in seeming delight as he drew near. "We only arrived ten minutes ago, and I feared you might have come before us and I would never find you!" Only then did he seem to become aware of her companions and nodded to them with noticeably less warmth. "Lady Platt, Sir Seymour," he greeted them politely.

As he turned back to Brie, his coolness vanished. "The first set is about to form. Would you do me the honour?"

Brie agreed and accompanied him onto the dance floor without a backward glance.

"Well! It will serve him right if I am unavailable later in the evening," declared Lady Platt to her husband. "Oh, no you don't!" she exclaimed, seeing him beginning to edge away. "You will dance with me *once* at least before you disappear into the card rooms for the night!" So saying, she led the reluctant Sir Seymour after her sister and the duke, contriving to be part of the same set.

As the dance ended, Lady Elizabeth came up, closely followed by Lord Garvey, who had been partnering her. Lady Platt, staying as near to her sister's side as possible, greeted her effusively.

"My lady, it is such a pleasure to see you again! I declare, you look positively *divine* tonight!" It was true, for her gown was a confection of white and silver which was especially becoming.

Elizabeth thanked her and returned the compliment politely before turning to Brie. "I so wanted to talk to you!" she said eagerly. "I saw you come in, but I was on the other side of the room and could not get to you before the music started. Pray tell me, how is the kitten doing?"

"He scarce has a limp now, and is already very affectionate," Brie answered readily. "I've christened him Velvet, by the bye."

"Why, that is perfect!" Elizabeth assured her.

At this point, several young men clamouring for the honour of the next dance with either Miss Gordon or the Lady Elizabeth successfully shouldered Lady Platt out of earshot, but she did not much regret it. It was apparently true that the Lady Elizabeth did not find Gabriella's excessive interest in animals vulgar, which was consoling, but that did not mean that she was required to listen to such drivel herself. She noticed that the Duke of Ravenham had not removed himself from her sister's side as of yet, and could not help but conclude, from his expression, that he was not quite repulsed by the subject, either.

The music started again and Lady Platt actually retired to the sidelines voluntarily (Sir Seymour having made good his escape) to watch the characters in this little play. Both Gabriella and Ravenham had taken different partners for this set, but she could not help but notice how often the duke's eyes turned towards her sister in spite of the obviously more beautiful young lady he was dancing with.

The stirrings of a faint, outrageous hope began in Lady Platt's unimaginative mind. Could the Duke of Ravenham actually be forming a slight *tendre* for little Gabriella? It seemed unlikely in the extreme, given the quality of the competition, but she supposed that stranger things had happened. The situation certainly bore watching; what a coup—for Gabriella, of course—if she could actually bring the duke up to scratch! She fell into a reverie at the thought of the benefits which would accrue to herself as a result of such a match.

"Need I ask who has claimed you for the supper dance?" Brie asked Elizabeth playfully during a break an hour or so later. "That will be your third with Lord Garvey, will it not?"

Elizabeth flushed prettily to the roots of her dark hair and nodded. "Oh, Brie!" she exclaimed, impulsively clutching her friend's arm. "Do you know, I actually think he may be going to propose!"

"Tonight?" asked Brie in surprise. She was well aware that a budding romance was in progress, but not that it had progressed so far!

"Well, probably not," conceded Elizabeth, "but before the Season is out."

"That shouldn't surprise me a bit," said Brie. "You must tell me right away when he does so that I don't lose a moment of happiness for you!"

"You don't think I'm imagining things, then?"

"Only in thinking he might wait till the end of the Season!" returned Brie, laughing. The music resumed then, and their partners approached to remind them of the dance.

Brie was enjoying herself enormously. She had actually seen very little of Angela and nothing at all of Sir Seymour, though she noticed her sister out on the floor for most of the sets, partnered by a variety of older gentlemen. Thankfully, Sir Frederick appeared not to be among the guests.

The only thorn in her side, and a small one it was, was Lord Timothy, who was every bit as persistent here as he had been at Almack's last week. She was careful to allow him only two dances, but that did not prevent him from pestering her for more, or from following her about whenever she was not actually on the dance floor. She was glad now that the duke had engaged her for the supper dance at the start of the evening, for she was beginning to find the role of goddess tiring.

Nor was he the only gentleman present to shower her with the most flattering attentions, though he was the most absurd. Many among the titled and wealthy seemed to find her one of the most charming ladies at the ball. She made the acquaintance of a few of those other charming ladies, as well, and had been invited to two different afternoon teas for the following week. Popularity had its advantages, she reflected.

Lady Platt was not impervious to the attention being paid her plain little sister, and though she wondered at what the possible attraction might be, she found it gratifying in the extreme as it could not but elevate her own social position by association; she casually mentioned her relationship to Miss Gordon at every opportunity. She had known that Ravenham's notice would be a good thing for Gabriella, but had never dreamed of this level of success!

It galled her to admit it, even to herself, but some measure of the credit had to go to Gabriella. It was gradually being borne in on her that her sister was neither so plain nor so dull as she had always thought her; certainly the gentlemen present didn't seem to think so! Lord Timothy had been pursuing Gabriella all night, and he was very nearly as wealthy as Ravenham, or would be when his father died. She must mention to her sister that the young lord was well worth cultivating.

The variety of dishes offered at the midnight supper was astonishing to country-bred Brie, and she enjoyed the food almost as much as the company. She and the duke were sharing a table with Elizabeth and Lord Garvey, and it made for a merry meal. After two days of thought on the matter, Brie had decided she was being foolish to condemn him on the basis of a single glance at a beautiful courtesan in the Park. As he now seemed willing to forget that piece of awkwardness for the moment, she found it

surprisingly easy to do likewise. Lady Platt, glancing over
at them from two tables away, would no doubt have been
disgusted to know that much of the laughter stemmed from
her sister's recounting of Velvet's antics.

The girls remained at the table while the gentlemen went
to fetch the ices offered for dessert, and Brie decided to
take that opportunity to speak to her friend privately.

"I'd like your advice," she began, "for I fear I may have
behaved rather badly." She proceeded to relate the story of
Sir Frederick's vicious attack upon poor Velvet on the day
that Elizabeth had helped her to doctor the kitten and her
subsequent desire never to see or speak of the man again.

"Then, two days ago, when he spoke to me so pleasantly, as if nothing had happened, I fear I lost my temper
and cut him dead. Your brother seemed most…surprised,
and I never did have a chance to explain my reasons to
him. Do you think I did wrong?" She refrained from
mentioning what had kept her from explaining, though she
still burned with curiosity about that black-haired beauty.
She wished she dared ask Elizabeth about her, but she
could not bring herself to do so.

"Not to my way of thinking," said Elizabeth decisively, "though I can't say for certain that most would
agree with me. After that story, I shall be tempted to cut
him myself. I know Dexter has never liked Sir Frederick,
and even warned me away from him once, though I still
don't know exactly why. I can't imagine that he would be
upset at your not caring for the man, though!"

Brie was about to remind her that the duke was yet unaware of Sir Frederick's cruelty to Velvet when her attention was caught by a bit of gossip being related rather
loudly at the next table.

"Needless to say, no one would receive her after that, nor her cousin either!" a turbaned dowager, unknown to Brie, was saying to a younger lady at her side.

"They learned quickly enough that Society has no use for upstarts and adventuresses! I don't know that she ever went so far as to *tell* anyone that her father had a great fortune, but I for one don't doubt for an instant that they themselves started the rumour. And then it turns out he is little better than a merchant, and a less than successful one at that! I ask you! But of course, this is last year's news. Fancy that you hadn't heard about it till now! It was quite an *on dit* in September, I assure you!"

The dowager went on to more current topics, avidly attended by her companion, but Brie sat as if turned to stone. Elizabeth had embarked on a rather long story about a cat she and Dexter had once had and appeared not to have noticed the other conversation at all, for which Brie was grateful.

"And then the silly thing could not get back down again!" Elizabeth said with a laugh. Brie did her best to assume an appropriately amused expression, though at the moment she was anything but amused.

An upstart, an adventuress, leading Society to believe she was high born and wealthy when she was not! Wasn't that exactly what she was doing? Of course she had never *schemed* to deceive anyone, but that did not mean that the polite world would be any more forgiving if—when—the truth came out. Which it would, of course, if she were to accept any offer of marriage she might receive, as her sister had been urging!

"Aren't they, Brie?" Elizabeth was saying, and Brie reined in her thoughts with an effort.

"What, Elizabeth? I fear I was woolgathering for a moment."

"Perfectly understandable, with all this noise," said Elizabeth. "I was merely commenting that kittens can be the drollest things."

"Oh! Certainly," replied Brie, recalling with difficulty what they had been speaking of before her devastating bit of eavesdropping.

The gentlemen rejoined them a few moments later, and the conversation moved on to other topics. The ices were as delightful as the other dishes had been, but Brie was unable to enjoy them properly; a pall had been cast over the evening for her.

IT WAS NEARLY TWO before the guests began to leave, and by the close of the evening Brie had nearly managed to regain her former high spirits, though she was beginning to feel the late hour. After all, if the Duke of Ravenham was willing to introduce her about, knowing full well her lack of fortune, how bad could it be? A tiny voice reminded her that he had no choice, as he had lost a wager, but she did her best to quell it.

After bidding an affectionate good-night to Elizabeth and a cordial one to her brother, Brie joined Lady Platt, who was about to go in search of her husband.

"He is in the card room, of course," she said resignedly. She wasn't angry, as she had long ago learned to keep herself amused at such dos without Sir Seymour's help. In fact, she had come to prefer it that way. "I only hope we shan't have to carry him to the carriage."

Before they could reach the hallway off which the card rooms and other small salons opened, however, the two sisters were waylaid by Lady Pinhurst, a handsome young brunette whom Lady Platt had met frequently until the past two years, when the Platts' social position had slipped slightly.

"Angela, my dear!" she gushed. "I vow it has been an age and more since I have seen you! We must arrange a meeting soon and have a real cose!"

"Certainly, dear Gwendolyn, certainly," agreed Lady Platt eagerly. Lady Pinhurst was a contact she very much wished to renew, as she still moved among the highest circles. "Pray come for tea one day this week."

"Indeed I shall," said Lady Pinhurst, before changing tack. "You sly thing! Here we all thought you had merely married into Sir Seymour's money, and all the time you were an heiress in your own right. And never a word from you about it! That shows real modesty in my mind, whatever Sally Jersey may say! Now why have you kept your dear little sister secluded in the country for so long rather than allowing us her company?"

"Our poor father could not bear to have her away from him," answered Angela, the very picture of the dutiful daughter. "But as he passed on a year and more ago, my mother and I thought it time dear Gabriella enjoyed the pleasures of a Season."

"Ah, yes. Your father was a viscount, I heard tonight. Have you a brother to inherit the title?"

At this point, Brie felt obliged to intervene, as it was increasingly obvious that Angela had no intention of correcting any of the woman's many misconceptions about them.

"No, my lady, I fear your informant was slightly mistaken," she said politely but firmly, ignoring Angela's warning shake of her head. "Our father was merely the second son of a viscount. His brother, who is still alive, is the successor, and he has two sons himself, so I fear our brother, Gabe, is hardly likely to inherit."

"Oh. Oh, I see," said Lady Pinhurst, less than pleased to have been in possession of inaccurate information.

"Well, that is neither here nor there, I suppose. Shouldn't hurt your chances in the least, my dear," she said kindly to Brie, "for word of your fortune has quite got about. And a pretty face, as well! I shall see you both someday soon! Ta ta!" She sidled away to share her newest tidbit of gossip with another dear friend.

"That was hardly necessary," Angela hissed as soon as Lady Pinhurst was out of earshot. "What possible harm could it do to allow people to think our father had the title? It's not as though he is still alive to contradict it!"

"Really, Angela!" exclaimed Brie, also in whispers. "How can you say so? It would be frightfully easy to disprove, I should think, and then how would we look to the world?" She knew this argument would carry more weight with her sister than a mere charge of dishonesty. She was right.

"Oh, very well, have it your way," replied Angela sulkily. "At least you had the wit to keep your mouth shut about your supposed 'fortune.' Come, let us find Seymour before we are the only ones left in the house."

CHAPTER TWELVE

"PINK FLOWERS for my hair, do you think, or would blue be better?" asked Elizabeth, holding out a spray of each for Brie's inspection. They had been spending a delightful morning shopping for fripperies, particularly for Elizabeth's fast-approaching come-out ball, which was now scarcely a week away.

Brie had nearly managed to forget her mortification over the gossip she had heard at Lady Bellerby's, and was taking great comfort from Elizabeth's friendship; Elizabeth knew full well that she was no heiress, even if Brie had not yet told her about her late father's profession. She vowed to herself that she would soon, Angela's strictures notwithstanding. She and Elizabeth had grown too close to keep such a secret from her.

"What colour is your dress to be?" asked Brie practically, concentrating on the business at hand.

"White, of course," said Elizabeth in disgusted tones. "You are so lucky you can get away with brighter shades. I daresay I could, too, with my dark colouring, but Dexter and Scottie, my old governess, insist that only white will do till after the ball, at the very least. Next, they will wish me to wait until I'm married to wear colours!"

"At least white looks good on you," said Brie comfortingly. "It makes my hair look quite drab, but seems to bring out the highlights in yours."

"But it is so ordinary! Everyone is wearing white this Season. Though perhaps you'll start a new fashion for colours as you have with your hairstyle. I dareswear I saw at least three girls wearing their hair long last night, though I know one of them for certain was wearing a hairpiece for the effect, for she had short hair but a week ago."

Brie ignored the latter part of this speech, though she knew it to be true, as the duke had once predicted. "We'll have to enliven your white with an unusual trim, I suppose. How about these peach flowers, or the pale green ones over there?"

Elizabeth finally decided on tiny amber roses for her hair and bought some lace edging in the same shade, which also happened to be that of her eyes. Brie thought the colour would enhance her "ordinary" gown admirably, and said so.

"Lord Garvey will be charmed, I'll be bound," she said teasingly. "How go things in that quarter, by the bye?"

"Well, but slowly," responded Elizabeth with a twinkle. "He keeps hinting, but has yet to declare himself. Do you think I dare hope?"

"Oh, dare away, darling," laughed Brie. "I see it as only a matter of time until you are the happiest of women, and he of men, for you are clearly besotted with each other."

"Is it truly that obvious?" asked Elizabeth, not completely dismayed. "Do you think Barry as besotted as I?"

Brie could assure her friend of Lord Garvey's devotion with perfect honesty, and the two girls continued their happy chatter as they went in search of yet another merchant eager to relieve them of their pin money.

"GABRIELLA, YOU WILL never guess what happened while you were out!" Angela greeted her sister on her return. Elizabeth had dropped Brie at the door, as she had another engagement that afternoon, and Brie was now relieved that she had not come in. Lady Platt's fine blue eyes shone with excitement and it even looked as though she might have run agitated fingers through her beautifully styled hair, if such a thing were possible.

"You're a very lucky girl, sister," drawled Sir Seymour, coming out of the parlour to join his wife in the hallway. "Let me be the first to congratulate you. Quite a conquest, quite a conquest." He seemed as pleased with himself as if he had been solely responsible for whatever triumph was being celebrated.

Brie noticed Madsen and his wife hovering near the dining room door, obviously eager to share in the good news which had befallen the family. Preferring that it not become below-stairs gossip before she knew what this news was, Brie indicated the parlour and shut the door once all three of them were within.

"Now, perhaps you can tell me what this great good fortune is that has befallen me in my absence. Has some unknown relative died and left me an heiress?" she asked jestingly.

"Even better," Angela assured her, "for you shall have both money and a husband."

Brie sobered at once. "What . . . whom do you mean?"

"Why, Lord Timothy Gardiner, of course," answered her sister, as if speaking to a slow child. "Do not say you knew nothing of this, for it is common knowledge that he has been your most persistent suitor. Has he not spoken to you yet?"

"Quite proper that he has not, my dear," Sir Seymour informed his wife. "I know it is becoming the fashion for young people to settle these things among themselves before consulting their elders, but it cannot be the wisest course."

The thought that Sir Seymour would disregard any fashion, particularly one he himself had embraced a few years ago, would have struck Brie as ludicrous if her mind were not completely taken up with the matter at hand.

"Are you saying that Lord Timothy came to make me an offer?" she asked, wanting to be very sure of the facts before proceeding any further with this discussion.

"Isn't that what we just said?" exclaimed Angela. Really, she would never have thought Gabriella could be such a slowtop! "I should think you'd be thrilled!"

"You didn't accept on my behalf, did you?" Brie was certain that this was not the usual procedure, but would not put anything past her ambitious relatives. "What exactly did he say, and what did you tell him?"

"Well, he asked for you at the outset, but when I told him you were out, he requested an audience with Seymour. Which, of course, I granted."

"He said that he had come to make you—his 'goddess,' I believe he said—an offer in form, if we would not think it presumptuous of him," continued Seymour. "Presumptuous! I ask you! With his fortune, and you having no dowry at all! I did not wish to appear vulgarly grateful, but I made it known to him that I had no fault to find with his suit."

"But you are not my guardian!" protested Brie, aghast that such a decision should be taken out of her hands.

"Sadly, no, and so I informed Lord Timothy," said her brother-in-law, pulling out a gold-chased snuffbox and flicking it expertly open with one hand. "Angela tells me, however, that you have been asking to invite your mother to London, and she can give her consent when she arrives. I cannot imagine that she will object to such a match."

"Have you written to her yet, Gabriella?" asked Angela when her husband paused.

"I—I have not yet posted the letter." Actually, she had not even written the letter, as Angela had never agreed to the invitation, and she had no intention of doing so now until Lord Timothy could be dissuaded. She had no doubt whatsoever that her mother's wishes would coincide with Angela's.

"Just as well. I'll write to her myself," Angela decided. "That is really more appropriate, anyway, as I am the one offering her hospitality."

So much for that reprieve, thought Brie.

"Please, say nothing of this in your letter," she pleaded. "I am not at all certain that I wish to marry Lord Timothy, and it would be cruel to raise Mother's hopes for naught." She was perfectly certain that she did *not* wish to marry him, but hoped that such temporising might deflect a pitched battle with her sister. It did not.

"Not wish to marry him!" Angela and Sir Seymour exclaimed together. Lady Platt silenced her husband with a glance and a quick shake of her head.

"Seymour, dear, perhaps you should leave us now. This is a feminine matter, and better left for us ladies to work out."

Sir Seymour obediently left the parlour and Angela turned to face her sister with a syrupy smile which caused Brie to brace herself.

"Dear Gabriella," she began, her voice as heavily honeyed as her smile, "it is obvious that Lord Timothy's offer has come as a surprise to you and that you need time to collect your thoughts. Perhaps I can help."

Brie decided that the time for mincing words was past. "No, Angela, it was not a complete surprise, as he has been mooning over me for more than a week now, though

I had no idea he meant to act so quickly. My thoughts are quite collected, however, and I can tell you at once that I have no intention of marrying him."

"Oh, I can certainly see why," retorted Angela sarcastically. "Why should you settle for a handsome gentleman of the nobility, with one of the most respectable fortunes in England, and who dotes upon you, as well? Any girl in her right mind would hold out for a better offer!" Her voice was as acid now as it had been sweet a moment ago. "Or—" a sudden thought seemed to strike her "—have you hopes of bringing Ravenham up to scratch? I must admit his title quite puts Lord Timothy in the shade, for he will be but an earl when his father dies, though their fortunes might be comparable."

"The duke has given me no reason for any expectations whatever," said Brie honestly, wondering why the very suggestion caused her heart to beat faster.

Her sister regarded her shrewdly for a moment. "No, I suppose that was a ridiculous notion. The Duke of Ravenham is far beyond your touch. But," she continued briskly, "Lord Timothy is the very next best thing, and far more than you had any right to dream of. What possible objection can you have to him?"

"I don't think I would like going through life as a goddess; Lord Timothy is no older than I am, practically a boy; and, of course, there is the minor fact that I don't love him."

"Love, pooh!" Lady Platt dismissed the poets' exalted emotion with a wave of her hand. "Very few people love each other before marriage, and precious few after, I am here to tell you. Though of course it can happen," she hastened to add, realising that she might be prejudicing her case. "And, of course, Lord Timothy already loves *you* to distraction, so you are halfway there already."

Brie saw that there would be no reasoning her sister out of her determination to see this match accomplished. From what she knew of Lord Timothy, she doubted that he would be any easier to convince. All she could think to do was to delay in hopes of…what? Who would come to rescue her? For some reason, her thoughts flew to the duke. But would this offer not mean the end of his irksome wager? He might well welcome the idea! Even to oblige His Grace, however, she had no desire to be placed on Lord Timothy's pedestal!

"Angela, I have the most frightful headache," she said suddenly. "Can we discuss this later?"

"I suppose so," said her sister reluctantly. Truly, Gabriella did look a bit pale. "Try to be down soon, though, for Lord Timothy said he would call again this afternoon to speak with you."

Brie was quite certain that her headache would last till evening, but merely smiled and nodded as she left the room.

Thankfully, Sir Seymour was nowhere in sight and she managed to reach the haven of the Blue Room unmolested. There she threw off her pelisse and bonnet in exasperation and flung herself into a chair. What a muddle everything had become!

Velvet, the kitten, awoke at her tempestuous entrance and regarded her curiously from the bed with wide golden eyes.

"You don't really want to know, do you?" Brie asked the cat. In response, Velvet leaped from the bed to her lap and curled up there, purring and kneading her thighs with his tiny black paws.

"Very well, then, I'll tell you all about it." Brie proceeded to relate the ups and downs of the past few days' experiences to the one creature she could trust to listen without criticising either her behaviour or her motives. Knowing that Velvet was no gossip, she then went on to describe her conflicting feelings for the Duke of Ravenham.

By the end of this lengthy recital, Brie felt much better and the vague headache she had exaggerated to her sister was gone—not that she intended to admit that, of course. Her confidant, having done his job, was asleep (in fact, most of his listening had been done with closed eyes). Setting the kitten carefully aside to avoid disturbing his well-earned rest, Brie rose to look out the window, as she had perceived the sound of a vehicle stopping.

Lord Timothy was immediately recognisable from above by his short stature and glossy black curls, which he wore *à la Grecque*. Brie quickly pulled a dressing gown over her frock and jumped into bed against the possibility of Lady Platt's attempting to force her downstairs.

This did not occur, however, Angela most likely feeling that she should make another attempt to reason with her sister before she could confront this inexplicably unwanted suitor. After perhaps twenty minutes, Lord Timothy took his leave, which Brie confirmed from her post behind the curtains.

Breathing more easily, she selected a book from the growing collection begun since her arrival in London. Thus far, all her acquisitions could be housed on a single shelf, but she felt that the quality of her "library" probably already surpassed that of Sir Seymour's downstairs. She had scarce had time to read a paragraph, however, when the sound of hooves stopping outside was repeated.

Going again to the window, Brie perceived Sir Frederick More descending from his horse. Curling her lip in distaste, she wondered what his business here might be; the usual flirtation with her sister, no doubt. Would he mention her behaviour toward him in the Park the other day? No doubt Angela would have something to say to her on that score!

As she stood by the window pondering such topics, she was surprised to hear the front door slam loudly, causing the entire house to reverberate with its force. Looking down, she saw Sir Frederick stride quickly to his horse, fling himself into the saddle and fairly gallop off down the street. He had stayed no more than three minutes.

Now what was *that* all about? Brie wondered with interest. But, as there was no way to satisfy her curiosity without curing her headache, she decided she could wait until morning—or at least dinnertime—to find out. By then there should be little likelihood of Lord Timothy returning to press his suit, depending, of course, on what excuse Angela had made for her absence.

Accordingly, Brie descended to the dining room at seven, the usual dinner hour at the Platt residence, cautiously dressed in a stay-at-home calico lest it be necessary to resume her role as invalid. She had decided to use the argument that should she accept Lord Timothy while the false rumour of her fortune still circulated, the Platts might well share in her disgrace once the truth became known. She somehow thought Angela would do anything rather than suffer disgrace.

Angela, however, did not immediately reopen the topic of Lord Timothy's proposal. "Gabriella!" she exclaimed upon seeing her sister. "So glad to see you feeling better. The most appalling thing has happened, I must tell you!" Her eyes glittered with suppressed excitement and Brie was hard pressed to tell whether her sister was happy or vexed about whatever news she was bursting to relate.

She was obliged to wait to find out, however, for at that moment Sir Seymour's footsteps were heard in the corridor and Angela put her finger to her lips. "Not a word now—I'll tell you after dinner," she whispered quickly before turning to greet her husband.

There was an unusual firmness in Sir Seymour's step as he walked to his place at the head of the table, and Brie noticed that the line of his mouth was almost grim—or as close to it as possible on such a dissipated countenance. He said nothing, however, merely nodding to his wife and sister-in-law as he seated himself.

It was a quiet meal, lacking the usual exchange of gossip between Sir Seymour and his lady, and Brie would have found it almost boring but for the fascinating play of expressions across her host's face as the meal progressed. While he was obviously deep in thought, Sir Seymour's features variously displayed determination, anger, uncertainty and, she thought, fear.

Lady Platt, meanwhile, ostensibly devoted her attention to her plate while casting frequent surreptitious glances at her husband. The tension in the room seemed to mount as the meal progressed.

When the last course was removed, Brie followed her sister out of the room with alacrity, anxious to hear what had occurred to so upset the routine of the household. Sir Seymour had not been sitting as long over his port lately as he had been used to, so she did not wish to waste any of the time that they might have alone.

"So stern he looks—who would have thought it?" Angela said as the door closed behind them. "I never knew he had such metal in his character! I vow I almost fear him in this mood!" Her eyes had lost none of their brightness.

"What has happened?" asked Brie, her curiosity rising even higher.

"Seymour ordered Sir Frederick from the house today! Can you imagine?" exclaimed Angela excitedly. "He was so forceful, Sir Frederick didn't dare refuse. I daresay *he* had never seen Seymour in such a mood, either."

"But why?" Brie felt strongly that Sir Frederick had no right to be welcomed under any roof in London, but she doubted that her reasons would be shared by her brother-in-law.

"Apparently Seymour heard some story linking Sir Frederick's name with mine and he went practically mad with jealousy," said her sister. "Isn't that the most romantic thing? You should have heard him! 'Get away from my wife!' he all but shouted."

Brie merely stared, hardly able to credit her ears, and trying to envisage Sir Seymour in a rage. Her imagination quite failed her.

"But now I fear he is going too far," Angela continued. "He ranted and raved for some time after Sir Frederick left, saying what a scoundrel he was to be pestering a married woman and giving rise to such gossip, and finished by saying that if he came near me again he would call Sir Frederick out! My Seymour!"

"Do you really think he would?" gasped Brie.

"I—I really don't know," replied her sister, more soberly. "In his present mood, I fear he just might. And Sir Frederick, I hear, is a crack shot, which Seymour certainly is not. What do you think we should do?"

"We?" asked Brie in surprise. "If you don't want Seymour shot, it seems obvious that you must avoid Sir Frederick's company. That should be simple enough, shouldn't it?"

"Not really," said Angela, "for we see him everywhere. Besides, he has been a very good friend, though I know *you* don't care for him. What I'd like to do is to convince Seymour that the gossips were completely mistaken—which, of course, they were," she added quickly. "Will you help me?"

"I? How?" Brie was frowning, having no desire to be drawn into the matter. Even the Duke of Ravenham had heard that particular gossip, she recalled. She only wondered that it had not come to Sir Seymour's attention sooner. Or perhaps he had finally worked up the courage to do something about it, now that he was drinking less.

"Speak to Seymour," said Angela eagerly. "Convince him that it is you that Sir Frederick has been coming to see and not I. After all, he did take you riding once, and even offered to mount you." She wisely refrained from mentioning the disastrous walk they had taken after that.

"Do you think I want *my* name linked with his?" Brie was outraged. "I'm sorry, Angela, but you'll have to think of something else."

"I had hoped it would not be necessary to remind you of all that I have done for you, Gabriella," said Angela with the air of a martyr. "I brought you to London, housed you, clothed you and introduced you to Society. Things have gone very well for you, you must admit. And all I ask in return is that you do this one small favour for me. It is not as though you actually have to associate with the man, you know. Just convince Seymour so he will not call Sir Frederick out and be killed." Angela actually managed to produce a small tear at the corner of one eye.

Brie was undone. She was well aware that her sister's persecuted pose was assumed, but there was much truth in what she said in spite of that. Angela *had* been the one to bring her here and had made her debut in Society possible, even if the Duke of Ravenham had been the one to bring her into fashion. If not for Angela, she never would

have seen the sights or the bookstores, nor would she have
met Elizabeth . . . or her brother. Since coming to London, she had begun to truly live, for better or worse.

"All right, Angela, I'll do it," she said quietly.

CHAPTER THIRTEEN

SIR FREDERICK MORE left the Platt town house in no very
amiable state of mind. Sir Seymour was not the first jealous husband to order him away from his lady, but he was
one of the unlikeliest. Who would have thought that fop
could have it in him? He would have to tread warily there
for a week or two, or possibly move on to new game, as the
beauteous Lady Platt had proved more reluctant than anticipated.

He had come there in part with the intention of inform-
ing Lady Platt of Miss Gordon's unladylike behaviour in
the Park two days since; having noticed that there was little love lost between the sisters, he thought he could trust
her to give the little upstart the tongue-lashing she deserved. He had also hoped to receive some of Angela's
customary flattery to soothe his bruised self-regard; the
two days he had spent drinking and wenching had not
helped in the least.

Twice now, Miss Gordon had flouted him: first in that
ridiculous matter of the cat, and then again in the Park.
She must not go unpunished, must not be allowed to make
the brilliant match she was obviously angling for with
Ravenham while she ruined his own prospects.

A nasty smile twisted Sir Frederick's handsome features. Yes, he thought he could pay her back in kind for
the insults she had handed him, since he was to get no help

from Lady Platt. He turned his horse's head towards White's and moved off at a brisk trot.

BRIE STOOD IRRESOLUTE outside Sir Seymour's library, chewing on her thumbnail. She wished with all her heart she had been able to think of some other, less distasteful, way to help her sister, but she had not and now she had to make good her word. Squaring her shoulders, she tapped lightly on the door.

Entering at Sir Seymour's command, Brie looked about her and her sense of the ridiculous reasserted itself, making her feel more at ease. The Platt library was for show, not for use, and was more liberally provided with statuary (both in quantity and quality) than with books. The volume her brother-in-law had open upon his lap had obviously come from a circulating library.

"Pardon me for disturbing you, Sir Seymour," began Brie, some of her nervousness returning, "but I must speak with you."

It suddenly struck her that she was in the absurd position of defending, for the second time in a week, the honour of a man she neither liked nor respected—detested, in fact! Perhaps it was some sort of penance. Sir Seymour was looking at her expectantly, however, so she forced herself to continue.

"Angela tells me that you have become very angry about Sir Frederick More's frequent visits to this house, and that you hold her somewhat responsible for them," she said tentatively.

"That blackguard! That scoundrel! That...I apologise, Gabriella, but what that knave deserves to be called, I must not say in a young lady's presence. But if you could hear what the gossips are saying about my Angela because of him! And yes, I fear she may have—innocently, of course!—encouraged him somewhat.''

Brie recalled the flagrant way her sister customarily flirted with Sir Frederick, even in her husband's presence, and wondered again how Sir Seymour could have been so wilfully blind for so long. But that was not her business here, she told herself.

"Sir, I—I feel I must tell you that Sir Frederick may not have come here wholly in pursuit of my sister.'' That much might even be true, she consoled herself. She would try to prevaricate as little as possible.

"What are you saying?'' Sir Seymour's head came up hopefully. He had been struggling for the past few hours to think of some honourable way to avoid calling the rascal out, and probably getting killed for his pains, but had come reluctantly to consider it his duty as a gentleman.

"Only that he has shown some small interest in myself, sir, and that I and not my sister might be the lure that draws him here so frequently.'' She hoped that Sir Seymour was not aware that she always managed to be otherwise engaged when Sir Frederick came to call, allowing him ample time alone with Lady Platt.

"You, Gabriella?'' he exclaimed eagerly. "Of course! I should have guessed it! And what more natural than that Angela should always be by to play propriety?'' Brie quickly coughed into her hand. "No wonder Angela became such friends with him. She was undoubtedly thinking of you all the time, such is her generous nature, and wished to cultivate him before ever you came to London.''

Brie thankfully saw that no further convincing would be required of her; Sir Seymour had obviously taken on that task himself. He chattered on for a few minutes in twofold relief at his wife's virtue and his own escape from the need to defend it.

"Still, I'm not certain you should encourage the fellow, Gabriella," he concluded. "He is nowhere near the match Lord Timothy is, you know. There are even rumours that Sir Frederick's gambling debts are piling up, though you would never suspect it to look at him. Take my advice, sister, and accept young Gardiner."

"Thank you for the advice, Sir Seymour," she said with commendable gravity. "I will consider it. I just wanted you to know how things stood before you, ah, made any other plans."

"It took courage to tell me, Gabriella, and I thank you," answered her brother-in-law. "You are a good sister to Angela, whatever she may say at times."

On this less-than-diplomatic speech, Brie left the room, glad to have the ordeal so easily over. She went in search of her sister, to report that her plan had been successful. "But, as Sir Seymour advised me not to encourage him unduly, it would probably be a good idea if he avoided the house for a while," she finished, and Angela reluctantly agreed. Hopefully a *very* long while, thought Brie privately.

AS HE HAD HOPED, Sir Frederick found Lord Garvey preparing to eat an early dinner at White's, as was his custom when he had not been invited elsewhere. Even more fortunate for his purposes, Garvey was alone; the confidences he intended could hardly be shared in front of a crowd.

"Well met, Garvey," he greeted the younger man as he approached his table. "Would you mind if I joined you? I also find myself without companionship this evening."

Garvey looked up in some surprise. He did not know Sir
Frederick well and had always felt a vague dislike for the
fellow, possibly because he knew that Ravenham, whose
opinion he respected, did not care for him. But, as he
himself knew nothing specific to More's discredit, he ami-
ably waved him to a seat. Certainly, the man's conversation must be preferable to silence or his own thoughts,
which wavered between gloomy and hopeful respecting the
Lady Elizabeth.

"By all means, Sir Frederick," he therefore answered
cheerfully enough. "I have only just ordered my meal.
There's old Gibson—let us wave him down that he might
bring our dinners together." They accordingly did so and
ordered, besides, a bottle of White's excellent claret.

"What do you here alone, my friend?" asked Sir Frederick, once the wine had been poured. He would have to
do his work quickly, as there was no knowing how long
they might have the table to themselves; any chance acquaintance might come in and interrupt them.

"No dinner invitation tonight, though I go to a card
party at Siskell's later on. And the cook here, I must admit, is better than the one I employ at my lodgings—
though that poor fellow may well simply be rusty from
lack of use, as I dine so seldom at home. Here, there is at
least a chance of conversation, as your presence demon-
strates."

"True enough," agreed Sir Frederick with a laugh, "and
my reasons are basically the same as your own. I had no
desire to be alone with my thoughts tonight."

This piqued Garvey's curiosity, as Sir Frederick had intended it to. "Anything you'd like to talk about, old boy?"
he asked cautiously.

"I doubt you'd care to hear my maudlin little tale," replied Sir Frederick. "Though I must admit 'twould be a

relief to share it with someone. But, I've no desire to bore you with what is no doubt a common enough story.''

"No, I assure you, I'd not be bored in the least. Pray unburden yourself, if you think you might feel better thereby. Was it a woman, perchance?'' prompted Garvey.

"Aye, isn't it always?'' asked Sir Frederick wryly. "It would be indiscreet to mention her name, as she moves—now—in high circles, but she was all in all to me upon a time. And still is, in truth, though she'll have nought to do with me lately.''

Lord Garvey thought with a pang of the gallants that constantly surrounded Elizabeth whenever they were in public, though he *thought* she favoured him, and was instantly sympathetic.

"Set her sights higher, has she?''

Sir Frederick grunted morosely. "Once, and not so long ago—only a few weeks, though now it seems years—she'd have overflowed with gratitude had I offered her my name. *Then* she was content merely with my protection, though, of course, I had every intention of, ah, regularising our relationship as soon as I could see my way clear.''

"Noble of you, I must say!'' exclaimed Lord Garvey in some surprise. It was virtually unheard of for a gentleman to offer marriage to his mistress; after all, where was the need? "You must have been exceedingly fond of her.''

"I was,'' sighed Sir Frederick, "and still am, though she has used me abominably of late.''

"You say she moves in high circles now. Do you mean she is actually accepted by the ton, and that they have no notion of her past, er, association with you?''

"That is precisely what I mean. A mere knight, though of noble stock, as I am, has no attraction for her now. She looks to be a peeress. Perhaps even, so I have heard, a duchess.''

Though he was not generally much of a gossip, Lord Garvey's curiosity was by now thoroughly aroused. He realised that this "lady," whoever she was, must almost certainly be known to him, if she had become as prominent as Sir Frederick claimed. Their meal arrived at that moment, but he was only momentarily diverted.

"But how could she have so thoroughly insinuated herself into Society without anyone knowing her background?" he asked, as soon as the waiter was out of earshot.

"There is little wrong with her background, save that interlude with myself that she would now, no doubt, sooner forget. And that occurred in Gloucestershire, before ever she came to London." A glance at Garvey confirmed that he had absorbed this casual clue. "She comes of good family and has a married sister in Town who was already established among the ton," he continued. "It was through her sister, a good friend of mine, that I became acquainted with her, as a matter of fact."

Garvey's usually candid eyes narrowed. He, like most of London, had heard the rumours linking More's name with Lady Platt's, and he formed a sudden unwelcome suspicion. And Dexter was a duke! They ate in silence for a few minutes, but Garvey could not let the subject drop.

"Does the lady in question not realise the risk she runs by snubbing you?" he enquired, still treading cautiously. After all, the reputation of one he had thought of as a friend might be at stake. "You could destroy her with a word. Does she not see that?"

"She trusts to my love to keep me silent, I daresay, though she has pushed me a bit far recently." His eyes flashed at the memory, which still stung, though not for the reason he was putting forth. "Still, I care too much for her to be the cause of her humiliation. If she can find happiness as Duchess of Ravenham, I shall not seek to prevent it, though it wound me to lose her.''

"Ravenham?'' asked Garvey sharply, his suspicion crystallising into certainty. ''Is the lady we speak of perchance Miss Gordon, Lady Platt's sister?''

"Please, please, my lord,'' admonished Sir Frederick in apparent anguish, "lower your voice, I pray. I was unforgivably indiscreet. You must not bruit this story about. I only meant to mitigate my suffering a bit by sharing it with another and I thank you for your forbearance in listening to my maunderings.''

He saw that Lord Garvey was still having trouble absorbing what he had just learned and deemed it a good moment to depart and let the seeds he had planted bear what fruit they might. He had been careful not to swear the man to secrecy, for fear that he might actually feel himself bound by such an oath.

"Well, it grows late, my lord, and I must hurry if I am to have time to dress for my evening engagements. Thank you again for sharing your table and your time.''

Garvey nodded absently as Sir Frederick took his leave. He was deep in a mental struggle. He was trying to remember everything he had ever heard about Miss Gabriella Gordon, the girl his Elizabeth called Brie. She counted the girl her best friend, she had told him so; had she been taken in by her? And Dexter...he seemed to be paying Miss Gordon more attention that was strictly necessary to fulfill the terms of their wager. That wretched wager! He himself was responsible for the two people he cared most about having their names linked with that of a possible harlot. Whatever was he to do?

When he rose some ten minutes later, he had come to a decision of sorts. He would closely watch Dexter's behaviour with Miss Gordon, to determine whether his friend was truly smitten, before saying anything. Besides, there was always the chance that Sir Frederick was being less than honest; his reputation, after all, was far from savoury. However, Garvey felt he owed Dexter too much to allow him to risk his life's happiness when he might be the means of preventing it. What luck that he had made no actual promise to Sir Frederick to remain silent! As Sir Frederick had asked, he would not "bruit the story about," but if he found Dexter to be serious about Miss Gordon, he would *have* to be told!

CHAPTER FOURTEEN

As BRIE DRESSED for the rout at the Countess Lieven's, her feelings were hardly those which might be expected of a young lady about to be received by one of the most influential women in London. Instead of a nervous flutter of happy excitement, she was conscious of a deepening depression of the spirits. Glancing at the window, where a steady rain beat against the glass as it had all day, she felt that the weather was appropriate to her mood.

This evening, the last of May, would mark the end of the Duke of Ravenham's agreement; after this, there would be no particular reason for him to seek her out or to stand up with her in public. *Unless he wishes to,* came the unbidden thought, which she quickly suppressed. After all, she told herself, the duke was not the only reason for her gloom.

Since Lady Bellerby's ball, Brie had felt increasingly that her rise in Society had taken place under false pretences. She was particularly concerned that the Duke of Ravenham, and, of course, Elizabeth might become implicated in any scandal created when—if—the truth about her father's profession and her lack of fortune became common knowledge. For that reason, she had resolved to tell the duke—tonight—of her late father's profession, lest he discover it first from another source. She had also resolved to be the first (if it was not already too late) to tell him of the rumours circulating that she was some sort of an heiress and, yes, that she had not disabused anyone of that notion last night when she had had the opportunity. At least she could console herself that *he* had never been deceived as to her financial standing.

The same could not be said of her father's profession, unfortunately. Why, oh why, had she not told him of that the very first day, when he could still have backed out of his bargain? She very much feared that the timing of her disclosure would make her look exactly like the scheming fortune-hunter he had taken her for at their first—no, second—meeting. Be that as it may, however, she would not put it off another day; she needed her sleep!

Though she had determined to broach these matters during the course of the evening, she had no idea how the information might be received. Would he cut her at once, as her sister seemed so certain he would? Or would he merely laugh and treat the whole as a joke? She had no way of knowing, but would soon find out. If only it did not matter so much!

"WE SHALL NEVER get inside before the dancing starts!" exclaimed Elizabeth worriedly, observing the long line of carriages ahead of them, each waiting to deposit its occupants at the Countess Lieven's doorstep. The weather, and the resultant state of the streets, only added to the delay.

"Afraid Garvey will already be engaged for the first set when you arrive?" teased her brother. That courtship seemed to be progressing nicely, and he had no fault to find with it. He never would have thought Barry would be such a slowtop, though! Obviously no understanding had been reached between them as yet.

He glanced sideways at Brie, who was unwontedly quiet. She was looking lovelier than ever, in a slip of white satin with an overdress of white net shot through with blue and green spangles, but something appeared to be troubling her.

"May I steal a march on the competition by claiming *your* first dance, Miss Gordon?" he asked, as much to bring her out of herself as to secure her agreement.

"What? Oh, yes, of course, Your Grace," she replied absently. She had realised that here, right now, was the perfect time and place for her confession and had been steeling herself to make it. She took a deep breath, but Elizabeth forestalled her.

"'Miss Gordon' and 'Your Grace'?" she mimicked. "I should think you two would be Brie and Dexter to each other by now!"

Both of them flushed slightly at her outspokenness, though in the darkness of the carriage Brie was aware only of her own embarrassment. Clearing her throat, she tried again.

"I would like to thank you both again for your kindness to me these past few weeks," she began, with the air of reciting a rehearsed speech. "I sincerely hope you will not have cause to regret it." Brother and sister were regarding her curiously by this time, and Brie felt her colour deepen as she forced herself to continue. Her heart was pounding now, and she wondered if they could hear it. If only she knew how they would react!

"There is something I—"

At that moment the door of the carriage was opened from the outside by the footman posted at the entrance to the Lieven mansion. They had arrived.

Brie was consumed by an almost overwhelming sense of relief that the moment had been postponed, followed by guilt that she had not spoken more quickly. Had she unconsciously planned it this way? she wondered. She stepped from the coach, her pulse slowing almost to normal, and renewed her resolve to speak before the evening ended.

"Don't worry," whispered the duke as they passed through the imposing portico. "Whatever you were going to say will wait, and it can't be anything worth spoiling your evening over." Brie hoped desperately that he was right.

IF LADY BELLERBY'S house had been an unexpected improvement over Almack's, Countess Lieven's left both in the dust. She had chosen fresh flowers as her "theme" for the evening, and had obviously paid well-qualified professionals to arrange them; the effect was that of a tropical paradise. It was absurdly easy to forget one was in a house at all and to imagine oneself in a marble-floored garden instead. Brie was completely enchanted.

"Your rooms are lovely, my lady," she told her hostess sincerely at the first opportunity. "I've never even had a dream so beautiful!" She spoke with the simple directness which was natural to her, with none of the gushing flattery so evident in most of the young ladies who were out to ingratiate themselves to this notable hostess. Countess Lieven was charmed at once.

"Thank you, my dear," she replied, all smiles. "It was in hopes of inspiring just such feelings that I had it arranged so. You make me feel I have succeeded."

"Oh, yes," breathed Brie, gazing about her in delight.

Countess Lieven moved on, telling various highly placed friends how lovely and well mannered she found Miss Gordon. "She'll do well this Season, you mark my words," she said later to the Princess Esterhazy, with the air of a prophetess.

Unaware of the boost she had just given her own social standing, Brie hurried to catch up with Dexter and Elizabeth, who had moved on ahead. Not at all to her surprise, Lord Garvey came forward eagerly to greet them, although the second dance was already under way.

"Eliza!" he exclaimed, all but ignoring her companions in his relief. "I had begun to fear you would not be here at all!" He clasped both her hands and gazed rapturously into her face.

The Duke of Ravenham cleared his throat at this point, causing Elizabeth and Lord Garvey to start apart self-consciously. "It is good to see you, too, Barry," he said drily, only one twitching eyebrow betraying his amusement.

"I fear the roads are worse than I had made allowance for. If you intended to lead my sister out for the next dance, you have my blessing." The duke wondered whether his phrasing might give Barry a hint. And why was the fellow suddenly staring so fixedly at Miss Gordon? The duke glanced at her himself, but could see nothing amiss. The music had stopped and the next set was forming, so both couples moved onto the floor.

There was no opportunity for talk for the next fifteen minutes, as it was a lively country dance, and Brie allowed herself to forget the task ahead of her and enjoy this moment of pleasure. To be sure, she had to admit she preferred waltzing with the duke above all else, but now she was just as glad such a chance for conversation was denied her.

The next dance *was* a waltz, but for that Brie was claimed by Lord Timothy, who had by no means given up his suit. He seemed to have resigned himself to waiting for her mother's arrival in London before receiving an answer, however, so he was not as importunate as she had feared.

Brie did not see the duke or his sister for quite some time after that, as every gentleman of her acquaintance seemed ready to partner her as soon as she returned from the floor. Though she managed to keep up a pretence of polite interest in whatever her current partner chose to regale her with, she was in reality deep in thought.

She was beginning to think that the easiest, though perhaps not the bravest, thing to do would be to make her confession to Elizabeth alone and to let her pass the information on to her brother later. Would it not serve the purpose just as well? The more she considered this option the better she liked it, though she knew she was playing the craven.

This decision made, she began to scan the room for the Lady Elizabeth, and at length she found her some distance away, dancing with a dark-haired gentleman whose name she could not at the moment recall. When the set ended, Brie tried to work her way through the mass of humanity (Countess Lieven's rout could be described as a most successful "crush") in the direction she had last seen her friend. Before she was able to reach her, however, the strains of a waltz began to play.

"Might I have this dance?" came a familiar voice from just behind her, and she swung round to look directly into the duke's grey eyes.

"I can't believe my luck in managing to find you in this mob just in time for a waltz," he continued. "Personally, I prefer the comfort of a room one can breathe in to social distinction, but I fear that is not the current fashion."

Brie was obliged to agree as they moved onto the dance floor. Her heart began to hammer again, as it had in the carriage. What excuse could she have this time for remaining silent?

"Elizabeth wanted me to inform you of the time of her come-out ball, as she neglected to do so. She would be desolate if you were unable to attend, I know."

They turned gracefully in time to the music as he spoke, but Brie was unable to properly enjoy the experience; his words had served to emphasise that she was here under false pretences. It was one thing to impose upon Society, but to her it seemed far worse to deceive these people who had become her friends.

"You are silent tonight," the duke observed. "You are still allowing something to bother you, I see." He was fairly certain that Brie was troubled by the fact that this was the agreed-upon last night of his "payment" and wished to set her mind at ease. He fully intended to continue seeing this unexpectedly fascinating young lady and wished her to know that, but he was unsure how to reassure her without having his motives misinterpreted. He chose a safe topic, hoping to work his way round to the subject he really wished to discuss.

"Elizabeth told me about your doctoring of Velvet, your kitten. I was impressed. Not everyone can handle a frightened cat without suffering harm in the process. Do you have a natural affinity for felines?"

His tone was light, but Brie felt her heart freeze within her. This was the moment! She had to tell him now!

"For all animals, actually. You see, Your Grace, my father—"

"Taught you extremely well," finished the duke for her. "He must have been a very talented veterinary surgeon. Was he educated here in England, or abroad?"

The shock she had received when she discovered he had recognised her from the Ruby Crown was as nothing compared to what she felt now.

"You knew? How... how long have you known?" The room seemed to suddenly take on an unreal quality, and not because of the flowers.

"For several weeks, actually," he replied, surprised at her stricken look. "After all, I had to know a *little* bit about the girl I was going to bring into fashion, didn't I?" His grey eyes twinkled teasingly.

Brie's knees nearly buckled beneath her, so overwhelming was her relief. In sudden concern, the duke tightened his grip upon her to keep her from stumbling.

"What? What is it?" he asked in some alarm.

Brie recovered her footing at once and continued the steps of the dance, nearly forgetting what had caused her lapse in the delightful sensation of being held so closely in his arms. The music seemed to engulf her, and she was barely able to resist an overwhelming desire to rest her head on his chest and tell him what she felt.

"Miss Gordon?" he was prompting, and she brought herself back to earth with a start.

"I—I'm fine," she managed to say. What had she been thinking of? "It is just that my sister seemed to think it would cause a scandal if anyone were to know of our father's profession." This last was almost a question.

"Hardly that," he assured her, "but still, we probably do not need to have it put into the papers. It is not as though we have told everyone that he was something else. We have just been discreetly silent on the subject."

"Lady Pinhurst thought he was a viscount," confessed Brie, ready to tell all now that the worst was over. "But I set her straight. I'm afraid she also assumes that I am some sort of heiress, though, and I was unsure how to go about silencing such a rumour."

The duke gazed at her for a moment in delight. He had not known such innocence and honesty could exist in feminine form—except in his sister, of course, and possibly his dear, departed mother (though he was less certain in the latter case). What a treasure this girl was!

"You really can't," he admitted after a moment. "If people wish to make unfounded assumptions, that is their right. After all, they can hardly expect you to introduce yourself by saying, 'Hello, I am Miss Gordon, and I have no dowry,' can they?"

"I suppose not," she conceded, with a reluctant chuckle at the thought of what reaction such an introduction might provoke.

The music ended at that point, and the duke suggested that they step out of one of the open French windows for a breath of air, "well within sight of the ballroom, of course. You may trust me to take better care of your reputation than you do yourself."

Brie regarded him suspiciously for a moment, suspecting a reference to Sir Frederick, but consented without making a retort. The evening was warm, but still much cooler than the overcrowded ballroom. Brie gulped in the fresher air gratefully.

"Now what was it you wished to tell Elizabeth and me in the carriage earlier?" asked the duke, leaning against the balustrade next to her.

The absurdity of her previous fears suddenly struck Brie forcibly, and she began to laugh. "I just . . . I mean . . . oh, never mind," she said between giggles. "It turns out it wasn't so important."

Dexter regarded her curiously, for he could see no good reason for such hilarity, but finally decided that it must be some private joke she had decided not to share. Vaguely hurt that she chose not to confide in him, he silently extended his arm to her.

"Very well, then," he said, more stiffly than perhaps he had intended. "I shall certainly not pry. If you have nothing to say after all, we had better rejoin the others."

Her eyes still dancing with amusement at her own expense, Brie nodded. She knew that the duke was offended, but decided that the lengthy explanation necessary could wait. Just now, she was so relieved to have the imagined ordeal so easily over—and with an actual promise of seeing the Duke of Ravenham again at his sister's ball—that she felt she was walking on air for the rest of the evening.

CHAPTER FIFTEEN

BRIE AWOKE the next morning with a marvellous sense of well-being; her worst fears had been laid to rest and she could look forward with pleasure to the rest of her London Season. She felt an outpouring of gratitude to her sister for inviting her here and to her mother for insisting that she come.

Her mother! Suddenly, she recalled that Angela had no doubt invited her to Town by now, and that her coming might well curtail her season by forcing her to accept Lord Timothy's offer. Now, more than ever, she was determined to stand firm against her relatives. Gabe, at least, would take her part! On sudden inspiration, Brie scrambled from under the blue counterpane and began to dress herself before her abigail appeared to help her some five minutes later, having been told by a chambermaid that there were signs of life in Miss Gordon's room.

Once downstairs, Brie lingered over her breakfast, waiting for her sister to put in an appearance. She seemed to be seeing less of Angela recently, she thought, though for the most part that was probably for the best. At any rate, Sir Seymour seemed to be seeking out his wife's company more and more often, and Brie hoped this might signal an improvement in a marriage which had stood in great need of it.

Now that she thought on it, her brother-in-law appeared to be drinking a great deal less than he had been a few weeks ago (and for the past few years, according to Angela), which might account for much of the change. When sober, Sir Seymour was almost likable, though still too dandified for Brie's taste.

These musings on the state of her sister's marriage were interrupted by the entrance of Angela herself. She hummed softly to herself as she loaded her plate from the sideboard, giving Brie further cause for speculation.

"Good morning, Angela," she said as her sister seated herself across the table. "You seem to be in excellent spirits."

"Yes, I suppose I am," replied Angela with an air of surprise. "Seymour and I went to the Glastons' dinner party last night, as you know, and we had a better time than I can remember since . . . well, for quite some time, anyway. And that even though we left rather early." This was said with a secret sort of smile which hinted that the best part of the evening had occurred after their return home.

"How nice," said Brie rather lamely. While happy for her sister, she had no desire to pry into the intimacies of her married life. Quickly, she changed the subject.

"Angela, I have been thinking. You invited Gabe to Town along with Mother, did you not?"

"Now why would I have done such a shatterbrained thing as that?" responded her sister. "What on earth would a fifteen-year-old child find to do in London at the height of the Season?"

"He might manage to make some connections which could be valuable to him later on." Brie kept her tone reasonable, fearful that Angela would completely reject the idea, in spite of her improved mood. "Of course, with him here, Mama might feel obliged to stay home with him in the evenings rather than chaperoning me about." She waited to see what effect this might have.

Angela's brows drew down in thought. "There is that, I suppose. It is not as though you *need* her as a chaperone to your fine affairs, you know. I can accompany you just as well."

"Of course." Brie's tone was noncommittal.

Angela's brow cleared somewhat. "I suppose there would be no real harm in it. As a matter of fact, since I did not specify one way or the other in my letter, she may well bring him, anyway, rather than leave him home alone with the servants. I can send off a note inviting him, I suppose."

Returning to her previous happy mood, Angela went on, "I can't help noticing, by the bye, that you have been receiving a flattering amount of attention from several extremely eligible *partis* in addition to Lord Timothy. If you are truly determined not to have him, perhaps I should give you some sisterly advice on how to bring a gentleman to the point. Have you made a choice yet?"

"No!" exclaimed Brie in alarm. "That is, there are still several more weeks in the Season. There is no hurry, is there?" At least it appeared that she was not to be forced to wed Lord Timothy against her will! With her heart still hammering in her breast, she realised that she *had* made a choice—but could see no real hope of bringing that particular gentleman "to the point". Somehow, she doubted that any of Angela's practiced wiles would have much effect on the Duke of Ravenham.

She had observed his behaviour closely at the ball last night. He had been perfectly amiable and attentive, but she had no real evidence that he felt anything stronger than friendship for her. Indeed, she had observed him behaving with equal, if not greater, gallantry towards one or two other young ladies, both more attractive (and undoubtedly more wealthy) than herself. With them, he flirted. With her, he discussed his sister and her cat—when he was not lecturing her about propriety.

Mentally, she shook herself. Did she not prefer it that way? She had often despised the coquettish wiles of the majority of young ladies "out" in Society; she was not about to join their ranks in order to "captivate" the duke—or any man!

"No, I suppose there is no hurry," her sister finally replied. "But it will not do to whistle a fortune down the wind just because you want to take your time, either. Take my advice, Gabriella—"

She was interrupted by a stentorous throat-clearing from the doorway of the dining room.

"Yes, Madsen, what is it?" asked his mistress impatiently.

"The Duke of Ravenham is without, enquiring whether Miss Gordon might wish to go driving this morning," he intoned. The presence of high nobility always intensified his pompously important air.

"Well, do not leave him standing on the doorstep, you dolt!" exclaimed Lady Platt. "Show him into the parlour and tell him we will join him in a moment."

"Yes, my lady," replied Madsen, leaving the room with unimpaired dignity.

"Did you hear that?" Angela turned to her sister excitedly. "He must have formed a *tendre* for you, Gabriella, for why else would he be here? Unless," she said, suddenly sobering, "it is merely to verify that the terms of his wager are up. But let us go and see!"

She left the room at once and Brie followed more slowly. Could Angela be right? Could the duke have possibly formed a *tendre* for her? As she remembered the number of beauties she had seen flocking about him on numerous occasions, it hardly seemed likely, but still, he was here....

"Good morning, Miss Gordon," said the duke cheerfully as she entered the parlour. "I am glad to see you so chipper after such a late night. I was just telling Lady Platt that you were the belle of the ball."

Brie blushed deeply. "Hardly that, Your Grace," she protested. "You are too kind." She noticed the speculative look Angela was giving her and rushed to change the subject.

"Did I understand correctly that you wish to take me driving, Your Grace?" Though he had given her permission to use his Christian name last night, she was not about to do so in her sister's presence, or she would very likely find an announcement in the papers the next morning!

"Did I not promise to give you another driving lesson at a later date, Miss Gordon?" The duke kept his manner strictly formal, as well, she noticed. "I am nothing if not a man of my word."

So that was it! Of course he would never back out of a promise he had made, though no doubt he had intended to complete her instruction before the agreed-upon term of the wager was completed.

"Oh, of course, Your Grace." She silently chided herself for her vague sense of disappointment. This was still more than she had expected, was it not? "I'll get my bonnet and be down in a moment."

IT WAS A SPARKLING morning (though now nearer to noon) for a drive through Hyde Park. The flowers were in full bloom and their perfume filled the air; Brie found it impossible to be anything but cheerful in such a setting.

"If you are going to trust me with the ribbons, Your Grace, it had best be while the Park is still relatively empty.

I cannot believe it will remain so for long on such a day,"
she said smilingly.

"Perhaps you are right. We don't want you careering
into another curricle now, do we?" he teased, knowing she
was already skilled enough to make such a mishap unlikely in the extreme—though even the best of drivers had
the occasional accident. "And now that we are alone,
perhaps we can revert to Dexter and Brie."

"Certainly," agreed Brie in the same spirit. "I can well
understand your wish not to be too familiar before my sister, for I share your sentiments fully." There—that should
assure him that she had no intention of forcing herself
upon him.

How fresh this girl was, how natural! thought Dexter.
As the Duke of Ravenham, he had, for the past few Seasons, been one of London's most sought-after *beaux* and
could have had his pick of several crops of young, hopeful beauties. But, though he had occasionally felt amusement, or even desire, when in the company of this or that
unexceptionable debutante, none had ever affected him
like this dowerless country girl from Gloucestershire, with
her love for animals and bright good humour.

He regarded her questioningly for a moment, as if trying to read her thoughts, but then shrugged slightly and
handed her the reins. "Let us see if you remember what I
taught you last week" was all he said.

For the next several minutes, Brie concentrated on her
driving, for she was conscious of a desire to gain the duke's
approval, if nothing else. Gradually, as the feel of the reins
in her hands grew more natural, she began to relax.

"Good," remarked the duke, breaking the silence.
"You were a bit tense at first, but I didn't like to say anything for fear of having the opposite effect to what I in-

tended." Then, to prevent that very problem, he changed the subject.

"You never did answer my question last night, you know," he said.

"Which question was that?" asked Brie, her eyes not leaving the trotting pair of blacks.

"About your father...ah, ah, relax your grip a bit. That's better. If you recall, I asked whether he received his education here or abroad."

"Oh, mostly abroad," replied Brie easily, now that her sudden alarm had subsided. She was not sure what she had expected him to ask, but this was not it. "You see," she continued, "the London Veterinary College didn't open until the early nineties, which was too late to be of much use to him, though he did come to Town to confer with Professor Saint Bel once or twice after the college was established. Of course, much of his learning came from experience with the animals themselves, which, I suppose, it must for most doctors, veterinary and otherwise."

"Very true," agreed the duke. He noticed that her driving was imperceptibly improving as she thought of other things. "I firmly believe that there is many a country housewife who is a better healer, given her raw experience, than the best-educated physician who has not yet had time to amass much practical knowledge."

They continued expounding their similar theories on that subject for some time, and then Brie suddenly recalled the obligation she had determined that morning to discharge.

"Your Grace...Dexter, did I mention that I have a younger brother?"

"Elizabeth told me, I believe. His name is Gabriel, after your father, is it not?"

"Yes, we call him Gabe at home. He wishes to follow in our father's footsteps—to be a veterinary surgeon, that is—and I promised before I left for London that I would do all I could while here to further his ambition. But I fear I have little idea what I might be able to do for him. Could you advise me, perhaps?"

"How old is Gabe now?"

"Fifteen."

"Has he been to school at all?"

"No, he's never been out of Gloucestershire. He did the rounds with father, though, just as I did, and has already acquired quite a lot of experience."

"Hmm." The duke considered the matter for a moment in silence. "I should think the best thing he could do now would be to go to one of the good public schools for a couple of years—Eton, perhaps—and then see about entering the London Veterinary College. I'll make some enquiries, in any event, and let you know. I fear I am hardly an authority on the subject."

"You're very kind, Your Grace. I really do appreciate this," said Brie sincerely, finally taking her eyes off the horses to favour him with a grateful glance.

A man could quite easily get lost in those eyes, thought the duke irrelevantly. "You are quite welcome, Miss Gordon, though I have done nothing as of yet."

They continued to gaze at each other, the horses slowing to a walk. It seemed to both that they were on the verge of some deeper understanding. At that inopportune moment, the duke became aware of the sound of rapid hoofbeats catching them up and glanced round. He immediately recognised the horse, a roan gelding, as one of his own and next realised that the agitated rider was his second groom.

"Hold up!" he said sharply to Brie, and within seconds the man drew level with them.

"Oh, Your Grace, thank the good Lord I've found you!" panted the groom. "It's Diana!"

Brie glanced quickly at the duke and saw an expression of anguished concern come over his face. Whoever Diana was, it was obvious that she meant a great deal to him. Could she possibly be the woman she had seen him with at the Ruby Crown—the one he had gazed at so longingly in the Park? A pang assailed her at the thought, but she did not have time to dwell on it.

"What is it, Stevens?" the duke was demanding. "Out with it! Is she hurt?"

"Not exactly, Your Grace. She's begun whelping, a full three days early, and she seems to be in trouble. I went for old Farrington, but he wouldn't come when he heard it was a dog, so I come after you."

"Fool! You shouldn't have told him which animal it was until he was already there!" Then, after a pause, "I'm sorry, Stevens, you weren't to know. Since the Prince had him doctor one of the royal horses, Farrington's been putting on airs and will see nothing but prime bloods. I'll come immediately; you had best go try to find another veterinary surgeon—or even a doctor, if he's not too high in the instep to take my money."

His face was drawn with worry and frustration as he took back the reins. "I'm afraid we will have to cut to-day's lesson short, Miss Gordon," he said, his voice gruff with emotion. "I'll take you home directly."

"No!" she exclaimed. Then, when he looked at her in surprise, she added, "I mean, there's no time to lose, if you want to save the pups. Is this her first litter?" The duke nodded, still somewhat bewildered at her attitude. "Might I come along? I don't mean to intrude, but I may be of some use, especially if your man fails to find another surgeon."

He hesitated for only a moment. "Certainly," he said with sudden decision. "Diana is the best foxhound I have, and if your presence might make the difference, I'd be a fool to refuse your help." Expertly turning the curricle, he whipped up the team and left the Park at breakneck speed.

CHAPTER SIXTEEN

DIANA WAS STRETCHED OUT on a pile of clean straw in an empty stall when they arrived a few minutes later. It was obvious even to the Duke of Ravenham that she was in distress, and Brie, who had seen whelping bitches in much the same condition before, knew at once that she had made the right decision to come.

"Quickly!" she said to the groom, who had followed them into the stall. "Get some clean linens and warm water. Also some string or twine. Your Grace," she said, turning to the duke, "might there be an apron or smock about that I can put on? This may be rather messy, and I would as lief not have to explain the condition of my gown to my sister. She did, after all, pay for it!"

"Certainly, certainly!" he exclaimed, hurrying away after the groom. He was not at all used to taking orders from young ladies, but his concern over Diana had thrust every other thought out of his mind.

Alone with Diana, a dainty black-and-brown foxhound, Brie first set about calming the bitch's fears and winning her confidence. Crooning softly, she laid one gentle hand on the dog's head and, with the other, felt along her side. There was no doubt that she was labouring to birth the first pup, and that something was preventing her from doing so; the very daintiness of the hound's build gave Brie a clue as to what it might be.

A few moments later, the duke returned with a grey satin robe over his arm. "Will this do?" he asked anxiously, holding it out.

Brie could not believe her eyes. That robe had no doubt cost twice what her own dress had! "I simply wished for something to throw over my gown, Your Grace," she said. "I should hate to ruin that lovely robe!"

"Oh, it is just an old one of my mother's," he replied, scarcely glancing at it. "No doubt it was overlooked when the rest of her things were given away. Please put it on. Didn't you say there was not a moment to lose? How is she?" He watched Diana worriedly as he spoke.

Brie realised that the foxhound meant far more to him than the robe possibly could, so she wordlessly put it on over her dress. "I'm not quite sure yet, though I have managed to calm her somewhat. Ah, there you are!" This to the groom, who entered at that moment. "Set those down here, if you please. Now, whom does Diana trust most?"

The men blinked at her in confusion before the duke said, "That would be me, I suppose. She is with me constantly, both here and on my estates."

"Fine," cut in Brie, not waiting for more details. "Would you come round here and hold her head then, Your Grace? Try to keep her calm while I make a quick examination."

The Duke of Ravenham obediently knelt by the dog's head, crooning to her much as Brie had done earlier. After watching him approvingly for a moment, Brie gave her attention back to the distressed bitch. With the duke at one end of Diana and Brie at the other, their two heads were nearly touching, though just now neither of them seemed to notice.

"It is as I thought," she announced after a pause. "The first puppy is a bit too large for her, and is breech, as well. She'll need some help to deliver it."

The two men exchanged dubious glances over her head, but as neither of them had the vaguest idea of what to do, they silently let her continue. Brie spread the linens under Diana's hips, then went to work. She considered using the twine, but discarded the idea for fear of harming the puppy, which might just still be alive. After a tense silence which lasted several minutes, she carefully drew out the tiny body and began to rub him vigorously with a scrap of linen.

"A dog pup, as I suspected!" she exclaimed with relief, as he began to breathe on his own as a result of her rubbing. "They are almost always larger than the females." Diana looked round in sudden interest and took over the cleaning process herself.

"She will probably be able to manage the rest on her own, but we will watch for a bit to be sure."

The two men nodded silently, awed by the miracle they had just witnessed. The duke had seriously feared that he would lose Diana, and the groom was fond of her, as well, for she was an unusually sweet-tempered dog.

"I—I don't know how to thank you, Miss Gordon," the duke managed to say after a moment. "By now, you probably have an idea of how much this dog means to me."

Brie smiled warmly at him, deeply touched by his concern for the little bitch. In her book, a man that could care so much for an animal had to be a good man.

"That horse at the Ruby Crown—you did not mistreat it, did you?"

He blinked at her sudden change of subject, but smiled and answered readily enough. "No, I had just purchased it from its owner, a brute of a tinker, to prevent its further mistreatment, as a matter of fact. But I seem to recall that you were in no mood to listen to explanations.''

"And you were in no mood to give them," Brie retorted, then stopped, suddenly embarrassed by the recollection. For surely the reason he had been so brusque was that she had interrupted his assignation with that woman, whoever she was.

The duke also remembered the reason for his ill temper at the time and was suddenly, uncharacteristically, almost as embarrassed as the girl before him. Now, more than before, he felt compelled to reassure her.

"I am not like to be in such a mood for such a cause again, Brie," he said quietly. Their eyes met over the busy forms of Diana and her new pup and again, as in the Park earlier, an unspoken understanding seemed to pass between them. Brie held her breath, waiting for the duke's next words.

"Dexter!" came Lady Elizabeth's voice from outside the stables.

"In here," he called, both frustrated and relieved at the interruption. What *had* he been about to say?

A moment later, Elizabeth appeared round the corner of the stall. "I came right down as soon as I heard," she was saying. "Poor Diana! I should never have gone shopping if... Oh! Brie! No one said that you were here!"

"We owe Miss Gordon a very great debt," the duke informed his sister. "If she had not come back with me, we might very well have lost Diana. As it is..." His voice trailed away, for Diana was again straining.

"Oh, dear!" exclaimed Elizabeth. "Are you certain she is all right?"

"Just puppy number two, I should think," replied Brie cheerfully. "We'll let her push on her own for a few minutes before doing anything, if you don't mind, Your Grace."

"You are the expert here, Miss Gordon," he answered quickly. "I would not presume to argue with you on the smallest point."

"How very pleasant," she teased, her turquoise eyes sparkling playfully. "I shall be sure to remind you of that at some future time."

He did not respond to her bantering tone as he might have, for he was still watching Diana with some trepidation. His worry proved needless, however, for in less than a minute the second pup had made its way into the world with no assistance from the human observers.

"As I thought," said Brie with satisfaction. "She should go on splendidly now. I suppose there is really no reason for us to remain, unless you wish to." She looked from the duke to his sister enquiringly.

"Oh, let us stay," cried Elizabeth eagerly. "I am simply dying to know how many pups Diana is going to have, and if I know Dexter he probably has at least one wager riding on the outcome."

The duke flushed slightly, and admitted this to be true. "If she has six or more it will be worth fifty pounds to me. Not from Garvey, obviously. He never gambles for mere money. In fact, Miss Gordon, it may interest you to know I have vowed never to wager with *him* again."

"Probably a wise decision," she returned calmly, deciding not to take offence, as no malice was apparently intended in his statement. "One never knows what kind of bumblebath a wager of unknown stakes might land one in."

Ravenham chuckled at her innocent expression and the three continued to converse lightly while waiting for Diana to complete her litter. One of the footmen brought sandwiches and lemonade at the duke's request and they made quite a merry party of it.

"Seven!" exclaimed Ravenham in obvious satisfaction some two hours later. "Do you think that will be all, Brie?" They had both grown comfortable with being on a first-name basis during their vigil, encouraged, no doubt, by Elizabeth's cheerful informality with both of them.

"Yes, she appears to be quite empty," replied Brie, palpating the little bitch gently. "And in excellent health, I might add, though she is no doubt exhausted. You might have someone bring her food and water right in here so that she won't have to leave the pups to eat."

"Gracious, I certainly am glad that *we* don't have seven at a time, aren't you, Brie?" commented Elizabeth as she rose and brushed the straw off her gown.

"But think how simple it would be to get a whole brood out of the way at once," returned Brie in the same vein.

"I still think I would prefer to have mine one at a time. What think you, Dex?" She turned to her brother with a roguish smile, hoping to embarrass him.

"As I shall never be in such a position, I feel no need to have an opinion on the subject," he retorted. He seemed to be avoiding Brie's eye for some reason.

"I must be getting back," said Brie regretfully. She could not remember when she had so enjoyed an afternoon. "I suppose I will have to explain my absence to Angela, after all. I hope she will not be *too* scandalised." Her expression was not hopeful.

"I'll escort you home at once," said the duke. "I will even come in to help you explain, if you think it might make things easier. I feel that to be the very least I owe you."

Elizabeth hugged her friend briefly, thanking her again for what she had done for Diana and promising to call on her soon. "I would accompany you, but I shall have to change immediately if I am not to be late to Miss Haverly's. I knew her in school, though we were hardly friends, and she has bidden me to attend an afternoon card party." She grimaced slightly. "I accepted the invitation, so I must keep my word."

Brie was still in excellent spirits when they reached the Platt residence a short while later; so much so that she cheerfully refused the duke's assistance. "I think it is time I began to stand up to my sister, Your Grace, don't you?"

"Bravo! I do indeed," he approved. "But please, I would prefer to remain Dexter, if you don't mind. That way I can continue to call you Brie, as my sister does, and I vastly prefer that to Miss Gordon."

She flushed with pleasure and agreed. "Thank you for the driving lesson, Dexter. Good day."

"We will continue it at a later date," he promised as he helped her to alight, though he knew full well that she was already more accomplished with the ribbons than most ladies of his acquaintance. "Good luck with your explanation. Don't hesitate to send for me if you should need reinforcements!" They parted at the doorway on the best of terms.

Brie entered the parlour a moment later, her head still high with her renewed sense of self-confidence. Lady Platt, already dressed for dinner, sat there alone with a ladies' periodical but threw it down the moment she spotted her sister.

"And where have you been till this hour?" she demanded at once. "Never say you were driving with Ravenham all this time! By the bye, I thought you once told me that it was the Lady Elizabeth who had offered to teach you to drive." Brie had never mentioned the earlier lesson to her sister, as it had ended so embarrassingly.

"There was a change of plans," replied Brie lightly, refusing to be intimidated for once. "Dex—the duke felt that he would be a better instructor than his sister."

Angela's eyes narrowed at the slip her sister had nearly made, but passed over it for the moment. "Are you telling me that he has been teaching you to drive for *four* hours? You must be quite the expert by now. Did you take tea in his curricle by chance?"

"No, in his stables, as a matter of fact," said Brie blandly. "That is where we have been for the last three of those four hours." She waited confidently for the outburst that was sure to follow.

"Are you lost to all sense of propriety?" Angela fairly screeched, exactly on cue. "I can think of absolutely nothing decent that a young lady might do for three hours in a stable! Were you seen, do you think?"

"Certainly, by several grooms, at least, and by the Lady Elizabeth," said Brie. Then, perceiving that her sister appeared to be on the verge of hysteria, she relented somewhat. "She was there as well, you see."

Angela visibly relaxed, realising that Gabriella's reputation, at least, must still be intact. "You still haven't told me what you were doing in Ravenham's stables for three hours," she pointed out a trifle more calmly.

"One of his prize foxhounds was having difficulty whelping, so I offered to help. Both the duke and his sister seemed very grateful," she added quickly, seeing that Lady Platt's colour was beginning to rise again. "I may very well have saved the dog's life, as their veterinarian had refused to come."

"And have you now decided to take up our esteemed father's profession?" asked Angela icily. "Really, Gabriella, have you no sense of decorum at all?"

"Not when an animal's life is at stake," snapped Brie. She had been patience itself at the start of this interview, but now it was wearing thin. "It would have been unforgivable in me to have done nothing, out of some mistaken sense of propriety, when my help could make a difference."

"Perhaps when I wash my hands of you, you can hire your services out to their friends," said Angela caustically. "Next you'll tell me everyone already knows that our father was a veterinary surgeon."

"No, I have only told the duke and his sister. And I must say that they did not seem particularly scandalised."

Angela glared at Brie, but realised that the damage could not be undone. "We can trust them to remain silent on the subject, I suppose," she said after a moment. "If you are discredited in Society it would reflect badly on Ravenham, as it was he who brought you into fashion. Don't be surprised if he wishes to see less and less of you now that he knows the truth, however!"

She saw the brief flicker of dismay on Brie's face and made a shrewd guess as to its cause. "Don't tell me you were actually hoping that he might continue to distinguish you now that the terms of his wager are over!" She gave a brittle little laugh at her sister's expression.

"Let me tell you, missie, that the Duke of Ravenham can choose among the wealthiest and most beautiful ladies in England for a bride. A nobody like yourself can be no temptation to him whatsoever. If he speaks to you at all after today, it will be strictly for his sister's benefit, as she seems to have taken a liking to you." Her tone plainly indicated that she was unable to fathom any reason for such an eccentricity on Lady Elizabeth's part.

Brie sat down rather suddenly. She had realised with a flash during her sister's lecture that she *had* begun to cherish a hope of engaging Dexter's affections, though she had not truly been aware of it before now.

During the course of the afternoon he had shown himself to be exactly the sort of man she had always dreamed of. Now that she knew the truth behind that mistreated horse at the Ruby Crown, she could not even use that feeble excuse to fend off her feelings for him. Here was a man whose love and concern for animals matched her own; that he was also the handsomest man of her acquaintance didn't seem to detract from his charm, either.

But she had no doubt that what her sister said was true. He had been grateful to her for saving his prize foxhound, but that did not mean he had any more tender feelings for her! Perhaps, however, if she could keep her own emotions in check, they could still be friends, she thought. They certainly had enough in common for just that!

She tried valiantly to allow none of her conflicting thoughts to show in her expression, and merely said to her sister, "You are quite mistaken, Angela. The Duke of Ravenham has been very kind to me, but I never expected that he might continue dancing attendance on me. Any fondness I feel for him is merely as Elizabeth's brother."

With that, she rose gracefully and left the room. Lady Platt's face showed plainly that she didn't believe a word of it, and Brie really could not blame her. She didn't believe it herself.

CHAPTER SEVENTEEN

"YOU SHOULD HAVE SEEN her, Barry! Not a bit ruffled, and she knew exactly what to do. I don't doubt for a moment that she saved Diana's life and, of course, this whole beautiful brood!"

"An impressive litter, I must say," agreed Lord Garvey with appreciation. They were in Ravenham's stables, where Dexter was proudly showing off the day-old pups to his friend. "I can't help but notice that you seem unusually taken with Miss Gordon, Dex," Garvey went on cautiously after a moment, worry creasing his brow.

"Yes, I—I suppose I am," replied the duke slowly, with a crooked smile. "Hadn't really thought much about it, I confess. I just like being around her."

Garvey watched his friend with concern; Ravenham was showing every sign of falling under the girl's influence. And it was only yesterday that Garvey had heard Sir Seymour defending his wife's name at White's by saying that it was his sister-in-law More had been seeing all along! Dexter would have to be told.

"Dexter, m'boy," he said heavily, "there's something I think you should know." He proceeded to relate the story Sir Frederick More had told him several nights ago. "I truly am sorry, Dex," he finished, "but, well, better that you hear it from me than elsewhere." He was already partly regretting his decision to speak after seeing the stricken expression on his friend's face.

"Do you mean it has become common knowledge? Is someone liable to tell me of it in some tavern, as well?" The duke was torn between disbelief and despair.

"No, no," Garvey quickly reassured him. "More told me privately, and asked that it remain so. Didn't swear me to silence, though, and I thought you should know—had a right to, in fact."

For a moment, the duke wished his friend had remained silent, that he had been left in blissful ignorance. But no! That was absurd. Sooner or later the girl's true nature would be bound to show itself. Suppose he had...had *married* her in said ignorance? Their union surely wouldn't have remained "blissful" for long! Still, there were things about this that he didn't quite understand.

"Why should More confide in *you*, of all people, Barry?" he asked. "You're an admirable fellow, of course, but you and he have never been boon companions, have you?"

"Good Lord, no! Scarcely know the man! He seemed rather cast down that evening, though, and I was probably the first available confidant he found. We must be glad it wasn't some gossipmonger instead of me, I suppose!"

"Hmm." The duke was thoughtful. He had never trusted Sir Frederick More, and would have liked to dismiss the story as an outright lie, but there were certain considerations which kept him from doing so.

"She cut him dead in the Park last week, did you know that?" he asked abruptly. "Wouldn't tell me why, either."

"Well, I have to admit that would fit," said Garvey cautiously, trying to gauge his friend's mood. "More said something about her pushing him too far of late. Said he cared too much for her to speak out in public, which is likely, but how long will he remain silent if she continues to cut him like that?"

The duke didn't think it likely in the least, but forbore saying so to Garvey, as it was obvious his sympathies for the moment were with Sir Frederick. He remembered the time in Hyde Park a few weeks ago when he had "rescued" Brie from a private *tête-à-tête* with the man and his disappointment was suddenly swallowed up in anger. Perhaps that's why she had seemed upset at his interference!

"You...you'd best go, Barry," he said absently. "I have a great deal on to think right now."

"Yes, I suppose you do," said Garvey, rising and leaving quietly. "Poor devil," he added under his breath.

The duke was scarcely aware of his departure. His disbelief was passing rapidly into certainty as he recalled past conversations with Brie which had puzzled him at the time. At the Countess Lieven's—there had been something she had wanted to tell him, then she had apparently changed her mind, in favour of discussing her father's profession. Might she have been about to confess her relationship with More?

His thoughts then returned to the episode in the Park last week. It all seemed to make sense in light of what Barry had just told him. No wonder she did not want him to call the fellow out! She was no doubt afraid that would bring everything out into the open. Or... did she secretly still care for Sir Frederick?

He recalled that it was not until after her social position was all but assured by her appearance at Almack's—and after he himself had shown more than a common interest in her—that she had so blatantly snubbed her erstwhile lover. To be sure, Sir Frederick could not compete with his own title or wealth; in fact, rumour had it that the fellow's gaming debts were beginning to get him well into dun territory. But surely there had been more promise in the looks which Brie had shared with him yesterday than mere eagerness to share his money and position!

The duke ground his teeth, furious that he should have been so easily duped by her seeming innocence. If he had been blind enough to actually marry the girl, she would no doubt have cuckolded him within a month of their wedding! He thanked God that his eyes had been opened in time.

Shaking himself as though to clear her from his thoughts, the duke rose and left the stables, which reminded him all too poignantly of what had passed between them yesterday. He called briskly for his steward and spent the next two hours attempting to immerse himself in the business of his various estates. At odd moments, however, Brie's winsome face would appear between the columns of figures and he would feel an almost imperceptible softening towards her, rapidly followed by another surge of rage.

After the third such occurrence he became aware of the steward regarding him curiously, as he had failed to answer the man's question regarding the drainage of some newly acquired acreage. Irritated at his inability to better school his thoughts, he abruptly dismissed his curious manager.

"We'll return to this later, John," he said brusquely. "I've other business to attend to just now." He rose and quit the room before the startled steward could reply.

Almost against his will he felt drawn back to the stables, where he and Brie had finally become friends and, yes, a little bit more than friends. Stopping at the stall of Mallow, the bay gelding that had been the cause of their first stormy encounter, he allowed his mind to return to that incident at the Ruby Crown Inn. He then recalled their next meeting, at the home of the Platts, and every other time they had been together, every word that had been spoken. Could she really have been leading him a merry chase the entire time? He doubted it at the moment, but quickly suppressed the feeling. She would not ensnare him again!

But what was he to do now? Now that he had momentarily controlled his rage and jealousy, he realised he had a decision to make. After all, he had been the one to bring her into fashion; he alone was responsible for the high place she presently held in Society. Must he therefore be the one to bring about her downfall?

While he doubted Sir Frederick's sentiment of caring for her—or anyone—enough to prevent his disgracing her, he realised with a shock that it was perfectly true of himself. Whatever she had done before he knew her, Brie had come to mean a great deal to him. More than that. Like a lightning bolt, the knowledge hit him that he loved her, deeply and passionately, and that this possible scandal had not altered that fact.

She would be at Lord and Lady Millingtons' tonight; he remembered Elizabeth saying so at breakfast. Well, he would not. Until he had time to thoroughly sort out his conflicting feelings of love and betrayal, Ravenham felt it best that he not see Brie at all. To do so might be to risk a scene, a declaration of either his devotion or his fury—he was not sure which.

Right now, however, he felt a need to forget, to blot her face from his memory for a few hours. There was a new tavern just off St. James Street which he had heard of. He would give it a try.

UPON ENTERING the large hall at the Millingtons' town house which would serve as a card room for the first half of the evening and a ballroom for the second half, Brie scanned the crowd already gathered there. The duke tended to be readily noticeable owing to his unusual height, but he was not in evidence. Probably not here yet, she thought, suppressing an irrational pang of disappointment.

"Well, Gabriella, are you up on the rules of *Vingt et un?* I hear that is the only card game Lady Millington considers worth playing," said Lady Platt, glancing about as eagerly as her sister.

"I'm certain I will manage," Brie replied. "After all, it is among the simplest of games." Sir Seymour had spent a half hour or so explaining this and one or two other popular games of skill and chance to his sister-in-law that afternoon, that she might not find herself at a loss come evening.

"No one has ever accused Lady Millington of possessing a first-rate intellect. Her husband is quite influential, however, and it will do none of us harm to be seen here. The stakes are to be low or imaginary, I have been informed—I hope for your sake that is true."

Sir Seymour looked somewhat disgusted at this news. "Perhaps some tables will prove to be more interesting than others," he drawled and ambled off in hopes of discovering that to be so.

Lady Platt spared him scarcely a glance. "Look, Gabriella, here comes the Lady Elizabeth! I wonder where the duke is?" she said in an undertone as Brie's friend approached on Lord Garvey's arm. Having finally become reluctantly aware that Elizabeth did not care overmuch for her, Lady Platt drifted off in the direction of the card tables as soon as they had exchanged greetings.

Brie thought Elizabeth seemed uncomfortable when she mentioned that Dexter would not be attending this evening, almost as though she were hiding something. And Lord Garvey was worse—he would not even meet her eyes. He led Elizabeth away before Brie could so much as ask after Diana's health.

Brie forced a smile to remain on her face. She had very much hoped to see Dexter tonight, as they had parted on such good terms yesterday. Was he intentionally avoiding her? Judging by Elizabeth's strained expression, it seemed all too likely. She reflected wretchedly that Angela must have been right, after all.

FOR THE FIRST TIME since meeting Brie, Elizabeth had been almost happy to escape her company. What could she possibly say to her? Dexter had spoken to her earlier that evening to inform her briefly that he would be dining out tonight and that Garvey could escort her to the Millingtons', as he would not be attending. When she had asked whether he had any message for Brie, she had been shocked at the anger and pain which contorted his face.

"No. No message," he had said tightly. Elizabeth could tell that he was holding some powerful emotion in check, but dared not question him further. He had slammed out of the house a few moments later.

She desperately hoped that whatever misunderstanding had occurred between her brother and her best friend might be resolved before her ball, which was now but two days away. She and Lord Garvey had reached an understanding during the drive here tonight, and hoped to announce their engagement on that evening. After the way Dexter had acted, however, she wondered if he might not find some way of absenting himself, as Brie was to be in attendance. That would spoil everything! She determined to force her brother to speak to her sometime during the next day, even if she had to tie him down to do it.

IN SPITE OF DEXTER'S absence and her own suspicions, Brie managed to glean some enjoyment from the evening. Cards were still novel enough to her not to seem at all dull, and she found that her luck seemed to be in. She mused to herself that it was rather a shame that the stakes were not real, as she would have stood to have made a tidy sum over the next two hours. Then, remembering the old adage, she reflected that she was no doubt equally unlucky at love and her spirits plummeted again.

As she rose to go in to supper, she was dismayed to see Lord Timothy Gardiner advancing towards her with a middle-aged matron at his elbow.

"Miss Gordon!" he called before he was within discreet earshot. "Might I hope to have the honour of leading you in to supper?"

Unfortunately, Mr. Harden, who had been sitting to her left and whom she had expected to partner her, had not yet actually asked, so she was obliged to agree.

"Splendid, splendid!" he exclaimed, still a shade too loudly. Brie wondered uncomfortably if he had been drinking. She hoped not; he was difficult enough to control when sober.

"Mother, is she not as exquisite as I told you? Miss Gordon, I'd like to present you to my mother, Lady Montrose." He gestured from Brie to the lady at his side, and Brie immediately dropped the appropriate curtsey to the countess.

"I am honoured, my lady," she said demurely, while toying with the idea of saying or doing something outrageous in front of Lord Timothy's mother as the easiest way of discouraging a match. Even Angela would hardly expect her to marry him against his parents' wishes, she thought cynically; they might possibly disinherit him.

From the hostile glare she received from Lady Montrose, however, it appeared that such measures would not be necessary. She nodded, as civility demanded, but spoke no word to her son's chosen one as they proceeded into the supper room. Her forbidding silence continued throughout the meal, casting a blight over the party, which also included Sir Seymour and Lady Platt.

Angela began in high good humour at the obvious reason for her ladyship and Gabriella sharing the same table, but it soon became evident to even the dullest observer that her sister was not in the countess's good graces. After a few attempts at polite conversation, she and Sir Seymour fell silent, leaving the burden of speaking to Lord Timothy, whose spirits seemed unimpaired by his mother's frigid manner.

"I trust I can claim you for the first dance, my divine one," he all but cooed to Brie in such an intimate tone that she blushed in spite of herself.

"No, I'm sorry, but I have already promised it to Mr. Harden," she was able to truthfully say, and was rewarded by a grudging flash of approval from Lady Montrose.

"The second, then?" asked Lord Timothy, undaunted.

Reluctantly, she nodded and the countess's face resumed its icy hauteur. Brie hoped that Lord Timothy's parents had more influence over him than was readily apparent this evening.

The rest of the party went smoothly enough, for she refused Lord Timothy more than the two dances propriety allowed for an unengaged couple and successfully parried all his attempts to get her alone, either in the garden or in one of the rooms set aside for those who preferred to continue at cards rather than dance.

There was no other opportunity for speech with Elizabeth, as she and Lord Garvey appeared completely absorbed in each other, and by the end of the evening Brie was both tired and frustrated. She recalled, however, that she was engaged to go to the theatre the next evening with Elizabeth and she hoped to contrive a moment alone with her friend to wring an explanation out of her, no matter how painful the truth might be.

CHAPTER EIGHTEEN

SIR FREDERICK MORE was getting tired of waiting. It had been a week since he had dropped his hints to Lord Garvey, confident that they would soon find their way to the Duke of Ravenham's ears, as Garvey was well known to be his best friend. But so far there was no sign that this had happened. Only two days ago he had seen Miss Gordon in Lady Elizabeth's curricle, which Ravenham would never have allowed had Garvey confided the story to him. Who would have thought a silly young buck like that could be so close-mouthed?

He looked about the cosy, exclusive pub he had chosen to while away an hour or two in cards and drink. Yes, there were several influential members of the ton present, although it was gone midnight. This place had become quite fashionable of late. Perhaps it was time to speed things along.

Rising casually from his chair, he sauntered about the room, looking for a likely group to share his "troubles" with. He settled on a table near the door at which were seated four highly placed members of the nobility, including the influential Marquess of Dunstable. More to his purpose, however, the group also included Lord Blenny, whose lady was well known as one of the leading tattle-mongers in Town. Anything uttered within her husband's hearing was sure to be the talk of London within twenty-four hours.

"Good evening, gentlemen," Sir Frederick said smoothly, drawing up a chair. "I find myself at loose ends this evening. Do you mind if I join you?" None seemed to object, so he sat down next to Blenny, his back to the door.

He took little part in the conversation at first, which ranged over a variety of such commonplace topics as the past hunting season and Prinny's latest waistcoat. Eventually, however, as Sir Frederick had known it would, the talk turned to the current favourites in the muslin company, including which lady was under whose protection.

"The beauteous Genevieve has gone to Melton, if you'll believe it," offered Lord Belknapp, a middle-aged roué who clung desperately to the trappings of more youthful dandies. "I'd have thought she'd hold out for richer prey."

Into the clamour of agreement and argument which greeted this tidbit, Sir Frederick quietly observed, "I find I prefer a bit of breeding in my, ah, companions. Makes for a generally more rewarding association."

The attention of his audience was immediately caught. Sir Frederick's exploits among the married ladies of the ton were all but legendary, though he and his paramours were generally discreet enough that little was known for certain.

"Is Lady Platt still high on your list of favourites?" asked Lord Blenny, who had had a drop more than was good for him. "Or are you looking to move on to some other poor blighter's wife?" He laughed loudly at his fancied perceptiveness. "If you're done with her, nod her my way. She looks to be a toothsome mouthful; always did fancy blondes." Lady Blenny was dark haired, and the only thing toothsome about her was her overbite.

"No, I found some time ago that dear Angela can't hold a candle to her little sister."

"Miss Gordon, you mean?" asked Dunstable incredulously, glancing over Sir Frederick's shoulder. "Bit above your touch, I would have thought; she's been moving in Ravenham's circle since the Season began." He was not a close friend of the duke's, but held him in the highest esteem. There had even been rumours that Miss Gordon might be in line to share his title.

"She is now," admitted Sir Frederick. "There was a time, though, not two months gone, that she wasn't nearly so high in the instep. Younger than her sister, of course, nearly as lovely, and a luscious armful in private. The young ones are always so eager to learn! Miss Gabriella Gordon was a pleasure to teach, I assure you!"

Before he could launch into his tale of recent abuse at Miss Gordon's hands, Sir Frederick was yanked roughly to his feet by the collar. A powerful grip on his shoulder turned him round and he found himself face-to-face with the Duke of Ravenham! He opened his mouth to say he knew not what, but was felled by a shattering blow to the jaw before he could utter a sound.

"Name your seconds," said the duke coldly as soon as Sir Frederick began to stir. The red fury which had momentarily overwhelmed him had passed, but the implacable set of his jaw showed that his rage still seethed below the surface, held rigidly in check—for the moment.

Sir Frederick struggled to a sitting position, wondering whether his jaw was broken. His mind flicked this way and that, seeking a way out of his predicament.

"Garvey will act for me," said the duke, when his adversary still did not speak. "Who shall I have him call on?"

"Ancroft. Harry Ancroft," he finally mumbled. "I'll speak to him before I go home tonight."

Sweeping the fascinated onlookers with an icy glare, the duke said, "I trust none of you will feel the need to repeat anything you may have seen or heard here tonight."

Heads shook to the accompaniment of muttered assurances, but Sir Frederick noted with some small satisfaction that Lord Blenny had already sidled out of the room. Miss Gordon would not escape unscathed!

After allowing the duke ample time to leave the vicinity, Sir Frederick departed the pub, saying no more to the assembled company than the duke had after his warning—which was precisely nothing. He hired a hack to take him to the Ancrofts' modest town house and was admitted without question by a slightly inebriated butler.

"T' master should be back soon, Sir Fred'ick," he informed the familiar visitor. "You can wait in the parlour 'f you wish."

Sir Frederick nodded and proceeded to the indicated apartment, hoping that his friend would not be too long. He helped himself to a generous measure of brandy to assist his vigil, but it was in fact less than fifteen minutes before Ancroft joined him.

"What's to do, Freddy?" he asked airily as he kicked the door shut with a negligent foot. "Finally decided to fly the country and wished to take your leave?"

Sir Frederick winced slightly, as this was precisely what he had decided to do during his short drive here. The only reason he had originally told his story to Lord Garvey instead of to the Duke of Ravenham himself was to avoid the very predicament he now found himself in. The duke was well known to be among the top two or three duellists in England, while Sir Frederick, in spite of a rumour to the contrary that he himself had circulated, was blessed with no more than average skill. Besides which, his debts had been increasingly nudging him towards the Continent these past few months. Better an exile than dead or in Newgate, he philosophised. But there was no need for his circumstances—or his cowardice—to become common knowledge.

"No, it's a matter of a duel," he informed Ancroft before his hesitation could be noticed. "I've come to ask you to second me."

EARLY ON THE MORNING of Elizabeth's ball, the Duke of Ravenham paid an unexpected visit to the Platt residence. Lady Platt was still at breakfast; indeed, most mornings she would be still abed at this hour, but she had been obliged to rise unusually early this day.

"Your Grace!" she said in astonishment upon entering the parlour, having left her meal half-finished when Madsen's amazing announcement had come. "I . . . we . . . did not look to see you here again."

"Yes, I know, my lady, I have been unforgivably rude in staying away, but I have come now to offer my apologies. Is it too much to hope that Miss Gordon will see me?"

"A great deal too much, I fear, Your Grace," replied Lady Platt, torn between sudden nervousness and lingering anger. "My sister is gone."

"Gone?" asked the duke sharply, warned by his hostess's tone that it was not a simple shopping trip being referred to. "When, where, and why?"

"At first light this morning, which is why I am awake to receive you at this hour," she said by way of reproof. Mornings were never her best time, especially of late. "I sent her home to Gloucestershire. As to the why, I find it hard to credit that you have not heard the gossip which is at this moment flying about London regarding her. Indeed, I rather assumed you had heard it before I did and credited it with your absence these two days past.''

"Are you saying that you condemned your sister solely on the basis of *gossip?*" he asked incredulously, with a fine disregard for the fact that he had done the same two days earlier. "Did you give her no chance to explain the facts of the matter?''

"What matter the facts?" demanded Lady Platt. "You of anyone should realise, Your Grace, that people will believe what they wish to believe, and that is generally the worst. My sister might be as pure and innocent as a new lamb, but her reputation is ruined nonetheless. I sent her out of this house before her presence here could ruin mine, as well!''

"You seem to be a very poor excuse for a sister, Lady Platt," said the duke blightingly. "It may interest you to know that when I heard Sir Frederick slinging his lies about two nights gone I instantly called him out because of it. The meeting was to have been at daybreak today, but the blackguard did not show. In the eyes of the world, that should go a long way towards exonerating your sister, as an honest man would never flee the field of honour.''

Lady Platt had the grace to look embarrassed. "I—I had no idea. I have not seen Frederick since . . . well, for several days, but I must admit that I thought the story improbable. As I had it from Lady Pinhurst, Gabriella was supposedly his, well . . .''

"Mistress," supplied the Duke.

"Er, yes. Before she ever came to London. But I know for certain that they had never met before that night at the theatre. Nor do I think Frederick had the wherewithal to keep any mistress, whoever she might be, though he lived rather well.''

Her eyes had been opened by degrees as to Sir Frederick's true nature, the final blow coming when she heard the story he had spread about her sister. In her chagrin at having been taken in by him, and for so long, Gabriella had borne the brunt of her anger, which should have more rightly been directed against Sir Frederick—or herself. She had already become somewhat ashamed of her treatment of her sister; it was now being borne in upon her that she might have committed a grave social error, as well, in sending Gabriella away.

"If you knew my sister to be innocent, why have we not heard from you ere now?" she asked, in a last attempt to defend herself by taking the offensive.

To her surprise, the great Duke of Ravenham, for all his vaunted wit, seemed momentarily at a loss for words. "I fear I have been as guilty as yourself, my lady, in condemning her unheard. It was only yesterday, after I had challenged Sir Frederick, that I sought to discover the facts. I owe my knowledge to my sister Elizabeth. She related to me an incident, which she had from Miss Gordon, in which More demonstrated his cruelty towards animals. I know enough of your sister already to realise that is one sin she could never forgive, and it quite explains her behaviour towards the man on one of our outings together. I suspect it was her cutting him in public which motivated Sir Frederick's nasty little story, in a twisted desire for revenge. Once I fully understood what had actually happened, I assure you I was far harsher on myself than I have been on you. It was with the intention of apologising to her that I came here today."

"So she cut him, did she?" mused Lady Platt, momentarily diverted from the problem at hand. "I wouldn't have thought she could carry such a thing off. She *has* come along, hasn't she?"

While the duke thought this sudden show of respect for her sister was no bad thing, he didn't feel that this was the time to dwell on it. "What time did she leave this morning, and how was she travelling?" he asked, bringing her ladyship back to the important issue.

"Nearly three hours ago. I sent her in my own carriage, of course; I am not completely without heart! Besides, I feared if she were seen leaving in a hired coach it might give rise to even more talk. What ought we to do, Your Grace?" She was by now assuming that he would help, and her hopes of a happy outcome were rising by the minute. A man did not defend the honour of a girl he cared nothing about!

"I shall go to fetch her at once. Do you tell anyone who asks for her that she is indisposed; it must not be known that she has left London if it can at all be helped, for that would but lend veracity to More's scurrilous lies. I shall try to have her back in time for my sister's ball tonight. You must go, in any even, to squelch speculation as much as possible." Lady Platt nodded acquiescence and the duke took his leave.

An hour later, having finished her interrupted breakfast, Lady Platt sat in the parlour again, working out the precise nature of the malady she would claim had afflicted her sister, should anyone ask. She had just decided that Gabriella was down with a bout of brain fever, brought on by the overexertion demanded by a first Season, when Madsen announced Lord Timothy Gardiner.

"My dear Lady Platt," he cried dramatically as he entered the room. "Pray do not tell me that my goddess has fled as a result of my importunities! Not for the world would I have driven her away from home and family; rather would I have withdrawn my suit entirely, painful though that must be to me. Or perhaps it was my absence yesterday which has brought about her flight. She may have seen it as a defection, though I swear that it was not!''

Angela tried desperately to marshal her thoughts. Lord Timothy seemed aware that Gabriella had gone, but unaware of the scandal which had precipitated it. She realised she must tread warily with him; there was always the chance that the Duke of Ravenham might not come up to scratch.

''Whatever do you mean?'' she asked innocently, hoping to discover exactly how much he knew.

''My mother told me she was seen leaving Town in your carriage, my lady, no doubt informed of the fact by one of her many spies. She seemed delighted at the news, thinking, I doubt not, that it would cool my ardour for Miss Gordon. Ever has she underestimated the strength of my passion, as I said to her when I agreed to her compromise.''

''Compromise?'' asked Angela, now truly bewildered. She wished to keep him talking until she could think of a plausible reason for Gabriella's departure.

''Yes, in return for my parents' promise not to disinherit me if I married her, I agreed to keep my distance for a week, torture though it be. They seemed to believe my ardour would cool were she not before me, though I warned them such measures would only strengthen my love. I finally agreed because it would be unseemly for my divine one to live in poverty. But now she is gone! I beg you to tell me that I will see my beloved again!''

Lady Platt was ready now, and answered easily enough. ''Of course you will see her again,'' she assured him. ''She is gone for only a few days at most. Our mother is coming to London, and preferred that Gabriella escort her hither in my carriage, so off she went.'' Until that moment, Angela had quite forgotten the invitation dispatched last week. She had not as yet received an answer to her letter, but hoped this excuse would work until she, or the Duke of Ravenham, could think of something better.

"Ah, your lady mother!" exclaimed Lord Timothy. "The one with the power to grant me my goddess's hand! I will leave you, then, to call again when that esteemed lady has arrived." Much relieved, he rose, bowed smoothly and departed.

CHAPTER NINETEEN

THE DUKE OF RAVENHAM, meanwhile, was galloping along the highway which headed northwest out of London. If Brie had a three-hour lead, he would need to ride full out if he were to overtake her before dark—and he had to! He had promised Elizabeth before he left to do everything within his power to be at her ball to act as host. He fully planned to be there, with Brie at his side. It would be a perfect opportunity to refute the raging gossip.

A chill drizzle began round noon, but rather than take shelter, he pressed on. Surely he would catch her up within the next two hours! He felt his discomfort was just; it helped somewhat to expiate the guilt he felt at having behaved so faithlessly towards the girl he had now determined to make his wife. Assuming, of course, that she would have him once she heard his confession!

The miles wore away under his horse's swift hooves. The rain trickled to a stop, and a pale gleam broke through the clouds, shining on an inn a short distance ahead. The Ruby Crown! It was yet only mid-afternoon, but he felt a surge of hope that Brie might have stopped here, as the place would be familiar to her. At any rate, he was feeling the need of sustenance to keep up his strength, as he had missed his luncheon, and this seemed as good a place as any to have a meal.

Reining in at the inn yard, he glanced about him. Could it have been only a few weeks ago that he had seen Brie here, for the first time? So much had happened since. His reminiscences were interrupted by the sight of a familiar crest on a travelling coach pulled off to one side of the main building. Sir Seymour's! She was here, then! Mentally preparing his speech, he tethered his mount and entered the inn.

BRIE SAT DEJECTEDLY over an excellent repast of roast mutton, bread, cheese and assorted fruits. For the hundredth time since beginning her journey that morning, she wondered what the future could possibly hold for her now.

Just the evening before, Elizabeth had assured her that her brother would soon come round, after reluctantly admitting that he had indeed been avoiding her. Her friend had seemed so certain that the situation would change, and soon, that Brie had allowed herself to be convinced. She had therefore not been prepared for the scene which awaited her at her sister's house upon her return from the theatre.

"Hussy! Harlot!" Angela had shrieked. "To think I have harboured such a viper in my bosom!" That ample portion of her anatomy had heaved with indignation. "Lady Pinhurst just left here, after telling me the whole sordid story!"

Though Brie had not known it, her sister's fury was largely fuelled by the smirking satisfaction her "dear friend" had taken in imparting the news. Angela's feelings found some relief in recounting her ladyship's tale word for word, as Gabriella's face paled with horror.

"Did you actually think you could keep such a secret from me—from Society?" Angela had asked when her tale was done.

"You know it isn't true! You know how I detest that man! And to think I told Sir Seymour he was interested in me—to protect you! Oh, Angela, how can you?"

Lady Platt had looked somewhat conscious at this reminder, but she was adamant nonetheless. She had sent two maids to help Brie pack and had bundled her off at first light.

And now she was here. She knew she could have travelled farther today, but when she had seen the familiar buildings of the Ruby Crown she had, on impulse, asked the coachman to stop. This was where she had first met Dexter, and it seemed somehow fitting she spend the night here, now that she was never to see him again.

Was it true, as Angela had said, that he had been avoiding her of late because of Sir Frederick's vicious gossip? It hurt her to think he would condemn her unheard, but it seemed the likeliest explanation. She rose from the table, her meal practically untouched, and looked about her.

This was the very same private parlour (she had the means to command one now) that Dexter had occupied before. Remembering that time, she thought again of the beautiful woman who had shared the parlour with him— but Dexter had all but told her that he no longer had any sort of a relationship with her, or anyone like her. Not that it mattered now, Brie reminded herself.

Sighing, she crossed to the door. Though it was only an hour or two past noon, she felt she would prefer to spend her remaining time here in her room (not the same one as before, but a much nicer chamber) trying to forget her troubles in the sleep she had been unable to achieve last night.

As she touched the doorknob, it turned under her hand. The door opened and she found herself looking up into the very face she had despaired of ever seeing again!

She gasped, and glimpsing the tender expression in Dexter's eyes, she suddenly found herself in his arms. Had she run to him, or had he pulled her into his embrace? She only knew that this was where she had longed to be—where she belonged. For one brief moment, all her troubles seemed to miraculously disappear, but then, reality intruded and she reluctantly disengaged herself from his grasp.

"How . . . how can you be here?" she asked, wondering all at once whether she might be dreaming after all. If so, she no longer had any desire to awaken.

"I came after you, as soon as your sister told me you had gone," replied Dexter. He had no more idea than she did how that sudden embrace had come about, but he suddenly felt that all his cares had fallen from him because of it. Even now, he caressed her face with his eyes, lingering on the soft fullness of her lips. But they were moving now, asking another question.

"Angela told you? Do you mean she sent you a message? Why?"

"No, I came to call on you this morning, at what I gather Lady Platt considered an unforgivably early hour, to apologise. I wronged you in my thoughts and, by avoiding you these two days past, in my actions, as well. For one who has always prided himself on giving no heed to the gossips, I have done a masterful job of allowing them to nearly destroy my life."

Brie scarcely heard the last part of his speech. It was enough that he now believed her innocent. Almost. "You might at least have asked me for the truth, Dexter," she couldn't help saying, her tone slightly accusing.

"Believe me, my love, you cannot castigate me any more harshly for that than I have already done myself. I called myself your friend, but I scarcely behaved like one."

Her feelings were thrown into confusion anew; first by the casual endearment he had used, followed almost immediately by the statement that he considered her but a friend! But even that was vastly more than she had dared hope for only a few minutes ago, she told herself.

"What...what changed your mind?" she asked finally, hardly knowing what she said. Was she his "love" or merely his "friend"?

"That tale will have to wait, I fear," he said, suddenly brisk. "I nearly forgot that we have need of haste! Elizabeth's ball is tonight, and I promised her I would be there, and you, too."

"Me?" gasped Brie, her eyes widening in dismay. "Will not everyone have heard that dreadful story by now? I could not bear to have them all laughing and smirking at me behind their hands." Angela had given her a very clear picture of the treatment she could now expect from Society. "Besides," she added, as though to clinch the matter, "Angela said I should never be welcome in her home again. Nor do I particularly wish to return there after the things she said to me. And she *knew* I was innocent! She had to!" Such thorough betrayal by her sister still stung.

"Lady Platt has had a change of heart," the duke informed her. "She will have told anyone who asks that you are indisposed. We can use that as your excuse if you really feel unequal to the ball, but I must say I expected you to have more pluck."

Almost instantly, Brie felt her back stiffen at that remark, as he had intended. "You are right," she said decisively. "I refuse to hide as though ashamed of something I did not do. I will not give Sir Frederick that satisfaction! I suppose it is too much to hope that he will be present?" She suddenly felt herself capable of knocking the man down if she saw him—and of enjoying it immensely! "And

I should hate to disappoint Elizabeth,'' she added as an afterthought.

The duke gazed down fondly at the girl beside him. He felt a strong temptation to say to the devil with the ball and remain here with her. As if she felt his gaze, she looked up to meet his eyes. Just as had happened twice before, something kindled between them. He lowered his head towards her upturned face. Both of them were breathing quickly.

Suddenly, a commotion in the hallway recalled them. The duke cursed himself for having neglected to shut the door and was moving to rectify that matter when a young, incredulous voice was heard to say, "Brie? Is that you?"

A slim youth of fourteen or fifteen strode into the parlour, followed closely by a middle-aged woman who had obviously once been quite pretty but was now rather faded and thin.

"Mother! Gabe! What do you here?" exclaimed Brie, torn between confusion, delight and a tinge of regret. She had been almost sure Dexter had been about to kiss her!

"Did you not know Angela invited us to London, dear?" asked Mrs. Gordon. She was pleased to see her daughter looking so well, but wondered at her presence at this inn. "We made good time today—we took the mail coach, you must know—and are here for an early dinner. It would have been more comfortable, I will admit, if your sister had sent her carriage, though probably not so fast." The look on her face showed clearly that such excessive speed hardly counted as an advantage with her.

Not so Gabe. "It's been famous, Brie," he said enthusiastically. "With all those horses that coach can fly like the wind! You should see it take the curves! I'm glad I managed to talk mother into it."

Mrs. Gordon's face took on a sickly hue, and Brie said quickly, "I'm glad you've enjoyed it so, Gabe, but now you can complete your journey in more comfort. I have Angela's carriage here, and we can return to London in it as soon as you may wish. Did she know you were to arrive so soon? She said nothing to me."

"No, dear," replied Mrs. Gordon, her colour returning at the good news Gabriella had just supplied. "I was so eager to see you both that I didn't wish to waste time with more letters back and forth. But—" her brow creased in perplexity "—if you did not expect to see us here, why have you left London?"

At this point, the duke, who had remained in the background during the reunion, came forward. "It is rather a long story, ma'am, and can serve to while away the return journey. I fear we must leave almost at once—as soon as you have dined, of course."

Mrs. Gordon regarded the handsome, elegant stranger before her with increasing approval. He was obviously someone of consequence. "Are you by chance Lord Timothy Gardiner?" she asked tentatively. Angela had communicated his flattering offer to Gabriella—and his financial status—in her letter.

The Duke of Ravenham's brows drew together, and Brie quickly came forward to make introductions. "No, Mother, this is the Duke of Ravenham. I believe I mentioned in one of my letters how kind he and his sister have been to me."

"Oh, so you are the Lady Elizabeth's brother! My Gabriella has become quite fond of your sister, I believe." Remembering her social training of many years past, Mrs. Gordon was able to smooth over the awkward moment as admirably as Lady Platt could have.

After exchanging a few more pleasantries, the duke went in search of the landlord to order meals for the Gordons and himself, for he had suddenly become aware of his own hunger again. His influence was sufficient that very few minutes passed before they were seated at table. He explained the need for haste as the food was served and Mrs. Gordon, having no wish to offend the duke or his sister, ate more quickly than was her wont. Gabe ate at his usual pace and finished before either of them.

"Shall I see about getting a fresh team for the carriage, Your Grace?" he asked, conscious of a desire to have this fine gentleman think well of him.

"Excellent idea, Gordon," replied the duke, knowing that a lad of fifteen would be much gratified by being treated as an adult. "I'll join you in a moment."

"I'll come with you, Gabe," offered Brie, feeling that she could tolerate no more small talk while her future hung in the balance. Action might settle her mind somewhat.

By the time the duke found them in the yard, the new team was already being hitched up. They looked like fine goers and he was now quite hopeful of reaching London in time for Elizabeth's ball.

"Would you mind if I drove?" he asked the ladies.

"No, not at all," they said, almost in unison. "The coachman can ride your horse back, if you wish," added Brie.

"My thoughts exactly," he replied. "Take it slowly, if you please," he said, turning to the coachman. "The poor fellow is tired and deserves a break."

"Yes, Yer Grace," answered the man. "I'll see he has some mash and a rubdown and a bit of a rest before we starts, if you prefer it." He was awed into better than usual manners by this dashing Corinthian.

"Excellent idea. Ladies?" The duke opened the door and assisted Brie and her mother to enter.

"Might...might I sit on the box with you, Your Grace?" asked Gabe tentatively, obviously fearful of a rebuff.

"I was just about to suggest it," replied the duke, to his delight. "Let us be off, then."

CHAPTER TWENTY

ELIZABETH WAS GROWING increasingly wrought. The guests were already arriving for the small dinner party which was to precede her ball and Dexter had not yet arrived. She had divined enough of his feelings to realise that he would not come alone if he could in any way convince Brie to accompany him, which she thoroughly approved of, but, oh! she wished he would hurry!

Barry looked at her questioningly as she stood conversing with Lady Carruthers, her great-aunt, and she shook her head slightly in response. He had called twice earlier that day hoping to speak to Dexter and thereby make their betrothal official so that it could be announced this evening; but, of course, her brother had been gone since before morning except for his one brief stop to assure Elizabeth that he would almost certainly be here tonight.

She forced herself to calmness and tried to pick up the thread of the wandering tale Lady Carruthers was relating. If the announcement had to be delayed, so be it. Brie's reputation was far more important than her plans for a memorable evening! And if all went well, she told herself, she might just end up with a new sister into the bargain!

Dinner was rather a trying meal, with Dexter's empty chair opposite her at the other end of the long table. She made a glib excuse that her brother had been called away on sudden business and told the company that he would no doubt be amongst them shortly.

"Hmmph!" snorted Lady Alicia, a needle-nosed woman whom both Dexter and Elizabeth detested, but who had to be invited as she was their late mother's first cousin. "Bad ton if you ask me, missing a dinner where one is expected to be host. Time he married and gave up this racketing about. I'll introduce him to Gwendolyn tonight if he deigns to put in an appearance."

Gwendolyn was Lady Alicia's husband's niece, a colourless, dejected-looking girl whom Lady Alicia had been trying to bring to the Duke of Ravenham's notice for the past month and more. Elizabeth couldn't help feeling sorry for the girl, as she sat staring at her plate in obvious embarrassment at her aunt's outspokenness, but could hardly wish her luck.

Dinner concluded without the duke's putting in said appearance. The ladies retired to the salon, closely followed by the gentlemen, as there was no host (or interesting conversation) to keep them at the table. Elizabeth glanced at the clock on the mantelpiece—the ball guests would be arriving in but ten minutes!

Lord Garvey, sensing her anxiety, moved close enough to speak into her ear. "Pray try not to fret, my love. If Dex said he would be here, you may rest assured he will move heaven and earth to keep his promise."

She threw him a grateful glance and smiled. "I am just a bit worried, Barry that is all. And a trifle nervous, I must admit. I hardly feel equal to the role I suddenly find myself in."

"You are equal to anything, sweetheart. I have total confidence in you."

The bracing words were not without effect, especially coming from the one dearest in the world to her. Elizabeth lifted her chin and straightened her back; she would make Barry proud of her—and Dexter, too, she vowed.

It was time. Lady Elizabeth Patton mounted to the top of the stairway where she would receive her guests with only the slightest tremour in the pit of her stomach. Any moment now...

"By Jove, Eliza, you look splendid!" came Dexter's voice, followed by Dexter himself as he strode quickly from the passageway which led to his rooms upstairs. "I daresay you could have carried it off by yourself after all. Don't know why I hurried."

He was every inch the fabulously elegant Duke of Ravenham, showing no sign whatsoever of the strain he had been through for the greater part of a long and extremely tiring day. His formal tailcoat of black fitted him as if it had been painted on and his intricate cravat gave the effect of a white linen waterfall. Every hair was carelessly in place.

Elizabeth breathed a sigh of relief and smiled at her brother, but before she could speak, the first guests were announced. The next hour was filled with introductions, curtsies, bows and compliments, a few of which were actually sincere. There was a brief respite round nine-thirty, and Elizabeth seized the opportunity to allay some of her curiosity.

"Quickly, Dexter, tell me what happened! Did you find her? Will she be here tonight? I vow I had almost despaired of seeing you this evening!"

"Yes, I did cut it rather fine, did I not?" He seemed almost pleased with himself, and Elizabeth's hopes soared, though she felt she could throttle him at the same time for so cheerfully putting her through the ordeal of the past two hours.

"I thought poor Matthews would have apoplexy when I turned up and told him I must be ready to receive guests in under fifteen minutes, but he did his usual flawless job, as I knew he would."

"Dexter!" Elizabeth was losing her patience, for more guests might arrive at any moment.

"Ah, yes. As to your first questions, I believe the answer even now approaches."

She turned to follow his gaze and saw Brie, resplendent in the rose satin the girls had chosen together for this occasion, entering on the arm of her brother-in-law. Glancing questioningly at the duke, she saw that he was frowning and guessed that he had not expected Lady Platt to absent herself.

"Were your sister and mother unable to attend?" he asked Brie after the formalities had been exchanged, earning him a startled glance from Elizabeth. Mother?

"Yes, m'dear wife asked me to convey her apologies," drawled Sir Seymour before she could answer. "She was taken ill—has felt poorly the past two or three mornings, as a matter of fact—and felt unequal to dancing. Mrs. Gordon offered to stay behind with her, lots of familial catching up to do, you understand."

The Duke of Ravenham nodded impatiently at the man and murmured something appropriate before turning a searching look on Brie who, however, seemed to be avoiding his eye. She curtsied most properly and followed Sir Seymour into the ballroom while the duke frowned at her back in perplexity. Now what was amiss with the girl? he wondered. There was no immediate opportunity to ponder on it, however, for another influx of guests, all from the very cream of Society, demanded his attention for the next half hour and more.

When at last he was able to leave his post, the dancing had already begun. Well, at least the papers would report the Ravenham ball as a success, he thought irritably, trying in vain to locate Brie among the brilliant moving throng. There! Was that her across the room with some blond-haired chap? But before he could be certain, a shift in the crowd obscured the lady from his view.

"Blast!" he muttered under his breath. Only this afternoon he had been so sure that everything was moving towards a quick and satisfactory conclusion. He began to skirt the edge of the dance floor in the direction of the lady who might have been Brie.

"Dex! Thank God you are here at last!" It was Lord Garvey, his face eager and relieved. "Where can we speak privately, m'boy? 'Tis most urgent, I assure you."

Casting a frustrated glance towards the far side of the room, the duke followed his friend into an empty salon off the ballroom which had not as yet been utilised for cards.

"What is it, Barry?" he asked with a touch of impatience when the door was closed behind them. His thoughts were wholly occupied with Brie and whatever her thoughts and feelings might be at this moment. He had intended to be at her side tonight, not to throw her to the Society wolves with no better protection than that simpering brother-in-law of hers!

"What is it?" echoed Lord Garvey incredulously. "Why, only that I wish to formally apply for your sister's hand in marriage! Nothing of importance, of course! Sorry to interrupt your evening over such a trifle."

The duke's attention was arrested at once. "Do you? Do you indeed, Barry! I was wondering when you were going to get round to it!" He slapped his friend jovially on the shoulder, his own troubles momentarily forgotten.

"Must say you gave Eliza and me quite a turn, being so late. She pretends it doesn't matter so much, but I know she has her heart quite set on being able to announce the betrothal tonight. And now, pending your approval, of course, she shall have her wish." It was clear that ensuring his darling's happiness counted above all.

The duke couldn't help smiling at Garvey's besotted expression. "You have it, of course. I was tempted to give it to you two weeks ago to save you the trouble of asking. You may tell Elizabeth that we can make the announcement at supper. And now, if you will excuse me, I have some unfinished business of my own to attend to."

"Are we to have a double announcement, Dex?" asked Garvey. He had noticed the duke's preoccupation and could make a pretty good guess as to its cause.

The look the duke gave him in response was enigmatic, and he left the room without replying, allowing Garvey to draw what conclusions he would—which he did, hurrying to share them with Elizabeth, along with his own good news.

It was after eleven when the duke finally succeeded in speaking to Miss Gordon. He himself had danced very little, doing so only because he knew that she was probably among those on the floor. Spotting her at last, he had the devil of a time getting close enough to attract her attention; he wondered suddenly if she had been deliberately avoiding him. When the set ended, he managed to draw her away from the young nobleman who had partnered her, and who was now solicitously offering to procure her some lemonade.

"I'll tend to Miss Gordon," the duke informed him curtly, "but I'm sure she thanks you for offering." Brie nodded uncertainly, but when she would have questioned him, the duke merely said, "Let us step out here, where we may talk uninterrupted for a moment."

Mutely, she allowed herself to be led through a curtained recess and found that they were on the balcony which ran the length of the house.

"Now," he said, once they were alone, "how have you been treated thus far this evening? Has it been as bad as you feared?"

"No, not at all," answered Brie, in surprise. This was not quite the question she had expected. "There have been a few raised eyebrows, some outright pity and lots of curious looks, but no one has snubbed me or laughed."

"And well they'd better not, in my home!" exclaimed the duke, his brows drawing down. Then he calmed himself, warned by her questioning glance. "I suppose Garvey did his job, then. Elizabeth told him to spread word to a few known gossips of More's craven behaviour; it would appear that the story has been got around. He was more than happy to oblige, she said. Seemed to feel it was the least he could do under the circumstances!"

"Yes!" Brie's head came up suddenly. "Why did you not tell me that you challenged Sir Frederick to a duel? That was surely a foolhardy thing to do—you might have been killed!" She remembered the horror she had felt when Angela had told her about the meeting which, thankfully, had never taken place. Then she remembered the other things Angela had said, and all her former diffidence returned.

The duke, however, was laughing. "Hardly likely, I think. In any event, his flight virtually saved your reputation, so I suppose we must be grateful to him, ironic as that seems. After all, I wouldn't wish my duchess to have any tarnish on her name."

Colour flamed across Brie's face. "Wh-what did you say?" she whispered.

The duke became suddenly serious. "I wanted to ask you at the inn, but we were interrupted. Miss Gordon, Brie, will you do me the very great honour of becoming my wife?"

She merely stared at him for a moment, her mind a whirl. Then, as if speaking to herself, she said, "So it's true what Angela said. You feel obliged to offer for me to save my reputation."

Angela had also advised her to nab him before he changed his mind, but, as much as she loved Dexter, she had no intention of allowing him to marry her from a sense of duty when he would so surely regret it later. She shook her head sadly.

"As I told you, my name seems to have escaped irreparable harm. This sort of sacrifice is not necessary. But I do thank you, Dexter; you have shown yourself to be a true friend."

With an odd, crooked smile Dexter said, "Gallant and lovely as ever. Do you really believe that to be my reason for proposing?"

Uncertainly, she gave a slight nod. "What else could it be?"

Stepping closer, he tilted her face up so that she was obliged to look directly at him. Once more, he was overwhelmed by the perfect beauty of her turquoise eyes. "This," he said, lowering his lips gently onto hers.

Brie caught one wondrous glimpse of the love and longing in his eyes before she was drowning in the sweetness of that kiss. Involuntarily, her arms went about his neck and she pressed herself closer and closer to him while their lips clung for an ecstatic eternity. One of Dexter's arms went about her slim waist while his other hand stroked sensuously up and down her back.

A tiny sigh escaped Brie's lips as he finally, reluctantly, released her. "I've wanted you to do that for ever so long," she murmured.

He chuckled with delight and surprise; not until that kiss had he been sure whether Brie returned his feelings. "Now will you consent to marry me?"

"I suppose I must," she replied, a charming dimple playing about the corner of her mouth. "Where else could I find someone who takes even better care of my reputation than I do myself?"

The duke threw back his head and laughed aloud. "You minx! Well, I suppose we have settled this just in time. Now we can announce our betrothal at supper along with Elizabeth's."

"Yes, isn't it marvelous about those two? She told me Lord Garvey finally mustered enough courage to ask your consent. Speaking of which, shouldn't you speak to my mother before we make a public announcement? She is my guardian, after all."

"I am aware of that, which is why I had the foresight to ask her blessing this afternoon while you were seeing to the fresh team."

Brie stared at him open-mouthed for a moment. "And she never said a word all the way back except to remark that you seemed a very handsome and polite gentleman! I thought she was sleeping for most of the journey, but it must have been a ruse to keep me from questioning her." She shook her head at such guile in her own mother. "It seems a shame, though, for her to miss the announcement."

"I told her I would try to arrange it thus. She must have felt she was needed more at your sister's side."

"Yes, she and Angela have always been very close—at least they were until Angela married and moved away to London. I hope she is not seriously ill."

"So do I, but I refuse to let such a worry spoil my evening—or yours. We'd best hurry if we are not to be late to supper. You don't wish to miss Elizabeth's announcement, do you?''

"Nor mine," said Brie with a rapturous smile.

They hurried to the supper room and reached it just as the last few guests were seating themselves. Ravenham stood in the centre of the room and cleared his throat a few times until he was certain he had everyone's attention.

"I'd like to take this opportunity to make a very happy announcement." Complete silence fell, as every person present regarded him expectantly. "Elizabeth, Garvey, would you please join me?"

They rose smilingly and came forward until they stood at his side. Brie stood somewhat behind them, trying to be as inconspicuous as possible so as not to detract from Elizabeth's moment.

"Lord Garvey, worthy man and friend that he is, has offered for my sister's hand and been duly accepted," began the duke rather pompously, then spoiled the dramatic effect by adding, "though he took his time getting round to it!" This produced a general chuckle. "Ladies and gentlemen, I present to you the newly betrothed Lady Elizabeth Patton and Barrymore Greene, Lord Garvey."

Applause broke out, along with nods of approval from all family members and many of the guests. The announcement had hardly been a surprise, but it was a nice climax to the evening, nonetheless, most were thinking. The duke allowed the congratulations to run their course before lifting his hand for silence once again. After several minutes, the assembled company obliged, though few expected that he might have anything else of interest to say.

"And now, one more announcement before you return to your suppers. I would like to introduce you to the next Duchess of Ravenham, my promised wife, Miss Gabriella Gordon." He drew Brie from behind him and held her close to his side with one arm. There was a startled murmur interspersed with a smattering of applause before Elizabeth spoke up.

"Dexter, you fox! You might have told me first! Oh, Brie, I'm so happy for you!" And in front of the cream of Society she embraced her new sister-to-be, while both girls shed a few tears of joy. That impulsive act set free the company's tongues and a clamour, mostly approving, arose. Only Lady Alicia left in a huff, her interested niece in tow, but nobody particularly noticed.

The two happy couples took their seats, long before the commotion at this unprecedented double announcement subsided, to have a cosy chat amongst themselves. They had barely started, however, before Brie felt a gentle hand upon her shoulder and turned to see her mother, with Sir Seymour just behind her.

"I'm so glad I made it in time to hear, my dear," she said warmly. "I'm certain you will be very happy."

"Oh, Mother," cried Brie, rising hastily to embrace her. Then her attention was drawn to Sir Seymour, who was taking his leave of the duke.

"I fear I must go to my wife immediately," he was concluding, which words would have alarmed Brie if her brother-in-law had not looked so happy.

"What is it?" she asked her mother.

"In a few months, you will become an aunt," Mrs. Gordon replied complacently. "Angela wanted me to tell Sir Seymour at once. It seems that I got to London just in time to settle both of my daughters' lives satisfactorily." And indeed, she seemed convinced that all had been brought about by her contrivance.

"I'll return with Sir Seymour now and see you at home later, or tomorrow if I am asleep when you return. I just wanted to be here to wish you happy, Gabriella." She took her son-in-law's arm and departed to be with Angela, extremely well satisfied with herself.

Brie watched her go with a smile. She and her mother had never been close, but it pleased her that she finally had her full approval—possibly for the first time in her life! Dexter touched her hand and she turned to see the love in his eyes, realising that her life from now on was going to be very sweet indeed!

Following the success of WITH THIS RING, Harlequin cordially invites you to enjoy the romance of the wedding season with

TO HAVE AND TO HOLD

BARBARA BRETTON
RITA CLAY ESTRADA
SANDRA JAMES
DEBBIE MACOMBER

A collection of romantic stories that celebrate the joy, excitement, and mishaps of planning that special day by these four award-winning Harlequin authors.

Available in April at your favorite Harlequin retail outlets.

THTH

HARLEQUIN PROUDLY PRESENTS A DAZZLING CONCEPT IN ROMANCE FICTION

One small town,
twelve terrific love stories

JOIN US FOR A YEAR IN THE FUTURE OF TYLER

Each book set in Tyler is a self-contained love story; together,
the twelve novels stitch the fabric of the community.

LOSE YOUR HEART TO TYLER!

Join us for the second TYLER book, BRIGHT HOPES, by
Pat Warren, available in April.

*Former Olympic track star Pam Casals arrives in Tyler to
coach the high school team. Phys ed instructor Patrick
Kelsey is first resentful, then delighted. And rumors fly about
the dead body discovered at the lodge.*

Take 4 bestselling love stories FREE

Plus get a FREE surprise gift!

◆ H A R L E Q U I N ®

A Calendar of Romance

Be a part of American Romance's year-long celebration of love and the holidays of 1992. Celebrate those special times each month with your favorite authors.

Next month, it's an explosion of springtime flowers and new beginnings in

APRIL						
S	M	T	W	T	F	S
			1	2	3	4
5	6	7	8	9	10	11
12	13	14	15	16	17	18
19	20	21	22	23	24	25
26	27	28	29	30		

#433 A MAN FOR EASTER
by Stella Cameron

Read all the books in *A Calendar of Romance*, coming to you one per month, all year, only in American Romance.

presents
MARCH MADNESS!

Come March, we're lining up four wonderful stories by four dazzling newcomers—and we guarantee you won't be disappointed! From the stark beauty of Medieval Wales to marauding *bandidos* in Chihuahua, Mexico, return to the days of enchantment and high adventure with characters who will touch your heart.

LOOK FOR

So rev up for spring with a bit of March Madness... only from
Harlequin Historicals!

MM92